A MANAGED SERIES PREQUEL

The
Seventh
Pawn

I0557965

Finlay Beach

The Seventh Pawn

For discounts on bulk orders of this novel, please reach out to Finlay Beach. Ideal for book clubs, educational use, or gifts!

Email: fin@openthegift.com

First Edition March 2024

eBook ISBN: 979-8-9857705-4-4

ASIN: B0CVFCD1D4

Print ISBN: 979-8-9857705-5-1

Audio ISBN: 979-8-9857705-6-8

10 9 8 7 6 5 4 3 2 1

Dedicated to Amazing Love

In memory of Faith and all who died suddenly.

Shadows of Rebellion

In shadows deep, the seventh pawn deftly rebels,
Shifting loyalty as royalty weaves its deceit.
With stealth and quiet commitment to truth,
He navigates unseen, allegiance skillfully reforged.
Within the turmoil, the subtle insurgent
charts his own course.

Chapter 1

HE GAZED BEYOND A dozen masts to take in the mesmerizing view of the Olympic Mountains with their snow-capped peaks and rugged terrain. This was the type of day his wife, Faith, adored. Even though the water spread out flat and the air hung lifeless, she would urge him, "Stop working so much. We have our dream boat, and it's time we use it."

Just her words, a gentle nudge, were enough for Julian to shut down his computer and join her on the deck. They would motor out of their coveted slip at Shilshole Bay Marina and aim *Horizon's Edge* towards the Strait of Juan de Fuca as if they were finally going to set sail into the Pacific. But each time, reality turned them back to their normal lives.

Their excuses echoed like a familiar refrain: "It's not time yet," "We have jobs," "Emily needs us for our grandson," and "Mom requires our attention—now more than ever." Despite these reasons or perhaps lurking apprehension, their dream of sailing the Pacific stayed securely moored at the dock. Escape seemed too audacious a venture. Yet deep within, Julian consciously ignored a secret—a truth potent enough to counter any one of those excuses.

When Julian was a boy, he learned how to deal with having the wind taken out of his sails. Each time they laid his dad off, his family moved to find a better job in a new city. New high schools had been a struggle, but in his senior year, he discovered his passion in a burgeoning movement—computers. The next disruption had nothing to do with his father's employment, it was solely due to Julian's inquisitive nature and his afterschool activities that altered his course forever.

As a seventeen-year-old, Julian found himself in the daunting spotlight of a federal investigation. The FBI raiding his bedroom and confiscating all his belongings was enough to convince him, but being labeled a notorious teenage hacker during the dawn of the personal computer revolution cemented his desire for an understated life. It was these tumultuous events that drove him to choose a life of quiet obscurity, a life lived deliberately below the radar. The second reason, equally compelling, was Faith.

Year after year, *normal* was his goal. Every week, Julian led a men's Bible study while Faith taught Sunday school. Working normal jobs, raising a normal child and living a normal life seemed easy. Until COVID changed everything. The government decided church gatherings were non-essential and his congregation was split over whether or not to comply with the lockdowns. The elders determined an *abundance of caution* was the most prudent course of action and the sermons were broadcast over the internet so nobody would die. While he missed his weekly gathering with friends, attending church online allowed for a degree of flexibility he enjoyed. The governor and the Department of Health shuttered far more than religious gatherings, but what did it matter to him? They seldom ate out. At least the grocery stores stayed open. He hated to shop, so retail closures meant nothing. He hadn't gone to a movie in years, and concerts were not the draw they had been when Springsteen was big.

Julian had to admit, a few months into the lockdown, the lack of his usual gym routines had softened his muscles. His monthly haircuts ceased, leaving his graying hair shaggy. Still, these were the limits of his suffering. With a reliable internet connection, he could work from anywhere and he enjoyed being home. Yet, he couldn't help but notice the toll the pandemic took on Faith. As a nurse at Harborview Medical Center, she silently carried the weight of her challenging role. Julian observed changes in her—a stoicism that bordered on detachment, especially when she spoke of the chaos at the hospital and the bureaucratic battles.

The streets of Seattle had also changed. The once-familiar city transformed into a landscape of apprehension, particularly after dark. Faith, a Seattle native, had always navigated the city streets with a certain confidence, but even her usual routes were tinged with an air of danger. The ambivalence of people was palpable, and Julian could sense Faith's unease, a silent acknowledgment that the familiar sidewalks offered too many shadows and no guarantee of safety.

After every shift, Julian met her at the staff door and they walked the short distance to their First Hill condo in silence. She'd take a long shower and cry. He could gauge the stress of her workday by how long it took before she finally emerged. At first, Julian tried to console her, but she shunned his efforts and said she needed time. As the virus spread, gunshots echoed, overdoses surged, domestic violence and suicides soared. She needed more time to grapple with the relentless tide of senseless deaths. But one day, it seemed that *time to sort things out* was not enough. She had reached her breaking point. "I'm going to quit. I know I'm only fifty-five, and yes, I've got six years before I can retire, but inside I feel I'm a hundred and five. Plus, I'm worried about Mom. People in nursing homes are dying! We need to get her out of there. It's time to bring her here. I'll take care of her myself."

"Faith, you know I'm supportive of you quitting your job. I've even suggested it before," Julian said, taking a seat across the dinner table. As he spoke, a twinge of guilt washed over him. Initially, his modest investment in Bitcoin seemed too trivial to mention, a small secret easily justified. But as the years passed and his speculation turned into a fortune, the weight of his secrecy grew heavier. The pretense of financial constraint had become a habitual facade.

The lie made him wonder if he had a spine, but the stacking of intangible cyber-numbers held little real meaning, so he continued. "Remember, we chose this smaller condo so we could afford to provide for your mom. With just one bedroom and the living room as my office—space is already tight." He paused, the words tasting of cowardice even as he uttered them, "Without your income, we'd be stretching our budget thin."

"Julian, we need to move out of the city and live somewhere safer and more affordable. You can work from anywhere and then I can take care of Mom. If we sell the boat we can afford it, and besides, Seattle is dying. I used to walk to and from work alone, even at night. Now, I need my own armed escort. Every day it gets worse. A girl died on my shift today. She was holding onto life and we thought she'd make it. They brought her in without clothes and no ID. A dozen lacerations on her body and blunt force trauma to the head." Faith wiped her eyes as tears flowed. "The thugs left her to die. Her body was so cold. . ." The tears stopped, and she rose from her seat with her hands pressed heavy on the table. "That could have been Emily!"

"I'm so sorry. I wish I could protect you from this kind of thing." He meant it as he stood to place an arm around her. "I agree. You need to leave your job, and maybe we should move, but don't you think we should pray about it?" She turned a shoulder to Julian forcing him to accept that any attempt to console her would be offensive.

"No! I don't think we should pray about it! I think you should just listen to me. The girl that died today? The hospital chaplain never left her side, and all the staff prayed. Look how prayer helped her! I'm done praying."

As Faith's remaining shifts at the hospital wound down, they walked hand in hand, back and forth, in brooding silence. But before her last day ever came to pass, something changed, and she insisted they go to the boat. "I've got a surprise for you," she said with a captivating smile and a youthful bounce in her step. When they arrived beside *Horizon's Edge*, she swept an arm towards their sailboat in an expressive gesture. "We can keep our dream. Abigail has agreed to take care of Mom during my shifts."

"That's nice of your sister. But you do understand, you just quit your job?"

"They offered me other work. It seems hiring nurses during a pandemic is all the rage."

"Where?" Julian asked.

Faith wrapped an arm around his waist. "That's the best part. Babies. I get to work with babies in the NICU. Plus..." she let go, backed away and spun around as if she were dancing. She settled with one foot in front of the other, then enunciated each syllable, "University of Washington Medical Center," and gave a theatrical bow.

"Your pension?"

"I'm still on track, different logo, same system. And... BABIES!"

"Sick babies," Julian corrected.

"Are you going to throw shade on this beautiful day, or are you going to kiss me?"

The recollection nearly brought a smile to his face. While there had been many beautiful days since, he steered his mind back to the familiar anguish that clung to him like a heavy burden.

Chapter 2

JULIAN REDIRECTED HIS FOCUS to the gentle swaying motion of his boat and the elusive freedom that teased him from just beyond his grasp. His phone vibrated—it had to be Emily since no one else made the effort.

"Hi, Dad. How are you doing today?"

"Just peachy. Like yesterday and the day before that and..."

"Why are you like that?" Emily interrupted.

"Like what?"

"Do we have to do this every day?" she asked.

"Do what?"

"Give it a rest! Dad, please, just get with the program, act like you care about something and move on."

"I hit the gym, showered, and even chatted over coffee with a regular. So, exercise, hygiene, and socializing. The only boxes I haven't checked today are eating and drinking water. And no, we don't have to do this every day, we could meet in person. I could take you and Asher out for ice cream. We could stroll and swing at the park like we used to."

"And what park might that be?"

"Green Lake is lovely this time of year."

"Really, Dad? When was the last time you walked Green Lake?"

"I'll admit, it's been a while."

"Maybe, like—2019," Emily said.

"That sounds right. Time flies."

"Uh, huh." There was a lengthy silence before Emily continued, "Please promise me you'll stick to the plan. And stay out of the parks, even the police don't go there anymore."

"The plan?"

"Yes, Dad, *the plan*. The same plan we keep talking about. The same plan everyone is supposed to be following. The plan that ensures a sustainable future for Asher and his generation—focusing on environmental preservation and community."

"I'm skeptical about that," Julian said.

"Yes, I know you are. But, please, stop following your hunches and listen to the experts for once!"

"Emily, we are being manipulated... again," Julian said, his voice tinged with a mix of weariness and sarcasm. "It's a power grab. They're using fear to keep us weak and obedient."

"You've been preaching that for years."

"No, I've been skeptical for years. I've only been trying to convince you for three hundred and ninety-four days."

Emily let out an audible huff. "Seriously, Dad, I miss her too, but life goes on, and it's way past time you give up your conspiracies. Your C3 score will take another dive, and you'll lose your boat."

"My boat isn't mortgaged. I own it outright," Julian declared proudly as his eyes swept over his floating home.

"You are special."

He noted a shift in her tone but couldn't decide if her intent was comforting or patronizing. Either way, he challenged her, "What do you mean by that?"

"When are you going to accept that owning things isn't helping? It's selfish," she said.

"Besides, family is automatically connected. If you cause trouble, some of it will rain down on us. Your actions will affect Asher. You could actually help improve his options in life if you fit in better."

"Is that what you're worried about?" Julian asked.

"Yes, and you should be too. And don't go all guilt-trip on me. You know I worry about a lot of things—you among them. I worry about your health, especially your mental health. It's okay to work through all the stages of grief, but you're stuck in anger. You need acceptance. They prescribed meds. Why do you keep refusing them?"

"Meds killed your mother."

"That's not true, Dad," Emily's voice softened, tinged with sadness. "She died of an idiopathic pulmonary embolism. It's hard, I know, but we have to face it. It's on her death certificate. You would know that if you actually dealt with her affairs. I thought I was doing you a favor by letting you grieve. Apparently, giving you time was the wrong thing. Let that conspiracy theory go. It's not based on science, and it's keeping you from healing and moving on with your life. What is it going to take for you to make more progress?"

"I thought you were an elementary school teacher. I never realized you moonlighted as a shrink."

"You might be surprised, but that's not the main issue. It's been over a year since Mom's death. You should have made more progress by now. You're expected to come to terms with it."

"I'm making progress daily. Even my trainer says I'm doing great for sixty," Julian noted, trying to inject some lightness into the conversation. "She even asked me if I was having sex regularly."

"Wow! That's good. I suppose you think that means she has the hots for you?"

"Yep. I sure do."

"Did you get a human personal trainer?" she asked.

"Nope."

"Oh great. You think you've got a chance with an AI fitness trainer who monitors your workouts? I can't wait. Can I be the maid-of-honor at your wedding?"

"I thought you didn't believe in gender stereotypes," Julian said.

"Say, when was the last time you went for a sail? Today is a nice day."

"Well, for one, there's not a lick of wind. Besides that, I've got work to do."

"Are you talking about university work or something else?"

"Not my day job, I don't get excited about that anymore. I'm only still working there because it makes you happy. But the world is my oyster, the cyber world that is. I'm off for the next four days, and have plans—there are bigger fish to fry."

"I think you're trying to irritate me, and it's working. Please don't make a mistake that could have serious consequences. You know they monitor us, especially online," Emily said, hinting at a past that Julian knew all too well. "It's for our safety—everyone's safety. It's the government's job to take care of us, and you need to respect that. Don't go looking into things that you have no business in. Please, Dad," she pleaded, "Your C3 score is important. They call it the Community Contribution Credit for a reason. Don't get leveled-down doing something stupid. Once should have been enough to teach you that lesson."

"Emily, I was paranoid before you were born, but it's refreshing to hear you understand what's going on. Surveillance is the way of the tyrant. That's why I'm exceedingly careful—especially now." Julian took a step down into the companionway and leaned his head into the shadow of the interior. "I'm careful. Like this call, nobody can listen in."

"You know you can get into just as much trouble evading surveillance. People go to jail for that. Jonathan and I have nothing to hide and we appreciate knowing someone is looking out for us. They are constantly doing their best to ensure our safety and preserve our planet for all generations." Emily paused and spoke slowly. "All I'm saying is to be careful about your C3 score. It is the key to our freedom."

"Is that the real reason you haven't had time to get together for the last two months? Not enough credit-juice to make it worth your while?"

"Dad, you're being a jerk."

Julian's voice grew colder, "And you're a pawn of the state that keeps you in chains."

"Why is it so difficult for you to realize C3 is important? Nobody's in chains." She took a moment before continuing, "We've got another week of school before a long weekend. I'll bring Asher and we can spend some time together."

Despite his better judgment, he couldn't help himself and said, "Sure, I've heard about the wonders of the Community Contribution Credit system and the Revised Capital Adjustment, but remind me how they're making things better? I'm just trying to see the bigger picture here." He sat against the slender top step. "Okay, I'm ready. Go for it. Convince me how complying with the whims of the state leads to a bright future for Asher's generation."

"Really?! You already know the good that has come out of the C3 score and the RCA. It's all working! We are building a better future together."

"Nicely done. You used C3 and RCA in a positive light—in the same sentence. Too bad they're not listening in on this conversation. It might have bought enough credit to compensate for an extra couple of hours of gaming time for your boyfriend."

The phone clicked off, and the cabin was suddenly filled with an oppressive silence. Julian leaned back, the weight of the conversation pressing on him as he stared blankly at the now darkened screen. "She's right. I am a jerk."

Chapter 3

THE UNUSUALLY LOW TIDE left a pungent odor of decay hanging in the air, a scent that would persist for hours as the invisible moon held the ebb tide captive. While even the slightest breeze would clear the air, the unseasonably warm day and the dead calm did nothing to change the smell, or his mood.

Julian's finger hovered over the call button. A tangle of apprehension and longing hung in his chest, before resigning to text Emily. He knew she would avoid his call. He typed, "Sorry," and pressed *send*. His gaze lingered on the phone, contemplating the relationship they struggled to continue. Silence would be easier to bear, but he loved his daughter and desired the close connection they used to have. Sliding the phone into his pocket, he would try harder. Next time they spoke, he would steer the conversation and talk about the weather, Asher, and avoid crashing into the rocks of his steadfast worldview.

The appeal of going for a sail was clear in his mind. Yet, the practicalities quickly lined up as deterrents—disconnecting his home, securing belongings, and navigating Port Authority permissions. Filing a computer form a day ahead of time was more bearable than speaking to a bureaucratic machine, but both methods demanded an excessive amount of detail about his boat, crew, destination, propulsion and even how he would prepare his meals. He also had to confirm he wasn't transporting people to another destination or involved in any commercial trade. The added carbon tax was not prohibitive, but an exorbitant fee to expedite the clearance on short notice insisted he consider if an impromptu outing was worth it.

The wind would pick up later in the day, as it always did this time of year. "Looks like a good day for sailing," he muttered, imagining Faith's agreeing nod. Reluctantly, he admitted to himself that being out on the water might bring some comfort to his soul, or at least give his heart a rest. With a rare four-day hiatus from his usual routine, the idea of casually cruising through the peaceful San Juan Islands appealed to him.

When Faith was alive, getting away from the rat race was all the reason they needed to set sail and cruise the Salish Sea. The expansive cruising ground presented endless possibilities for adventure. Escaping for weeks on end had always been part of their dream. Faith had loved whale watching, sightseeing and visiting with boaters. She would say, "Let's go to Friday Harbor." Ducking in and out of the quaint shops had been part of the fun, but most of the time, she wanted to sail or languish on the hook. Their days were spent reading, cooking and watching the kingfishers in their purposeful pursuits and the eagles and osprey commanding the sky. Sometimes Faith would fish off the boat's swim platform, but during the season, she'd rather take the dinghy to shore and dig clams or throw a dip-net over the side and catch Dungeness crab.

The pandemic altered everything. Once the consensus formed that "two weeks to flatten the curve" was a reasonable approach, government restrictions swiftly ensued, fundamentally transforming life. The fleeting impulse to sail to Sucia Island flickered and died as quickly as it sparked, leaving him anchored in the flotsam of memories. Faith had died, and everything else had changed as well. Clamming and crabbing were a thing of the past. The hard-shelled creatures were still down there, but once they had designated the Salish Sea as a World Marine Preserve it became illegal to harvest them. Keeping up with the fishing limitations and regulations robbed any satisfaction out of the process as well. And while the kingfishers and osprey appeared to have enough food, the eagles seemed to miss the human obsession to pull food from the deep. The eagles adapted, but quarreled more—irritated that man had created a new normal for them as well.

Julian yearned for a way to adapt like the birds had, where life and death were mere facts, a state of existence where he could live fully in the present, unshackled by the past and unconcerned about the future. He longed to rediscover this natural equilibrium, a balance that now felt agonizingly distant. He recognized that the innate human connection with nature was a relic of the past, lost somewhere in the Garden. Now, in his present state of turmoil, he found himself despising *the new normal*, and the smell of the air around him only further tainted his mood.

Horizon's Edge had only left her slip once since Faith's death—for her memorial—embarking on a daysail to the eastern fringe of the Strait of Juan de Fuca, nestled between the Olympic Peninsula and Whidbey Island. The day proved dismal for sailing—sluggish air, and dreary skies. Even the current wasn't ideal for the voyage. Julian, though dutifully assuming the role of captain, bore a disingenuous demeanor that belied the true Celebration of Life. Emily, not yet thirty, cradled Asher on the deck, while Jonathan remained below. Faith's sister, Abigail, undertook the daunting task of comforting their mother, who seemed disconnected from reality. It was difficult to discern if his mother-in-law even grasped the fact that she had lost a daughter, her gaze vacant and distant. As Julian guided the sailboat along its predetermined compass bearing, Abigail whispered a prayer. Julian silently mouthed *Amen*. Emily gently lowered Faith's ashes into the cold, dark water. He turned the large wheel, hand over hand, abandoning the compass course, heading the boat towards Point-No-Point. Irony struck him as he contemplated the name of the navigation light, wondering if it might serve as a metaphor for his own life.

The old quote, *a ship in harbor is safe, but that is not what ships are built for,* darted through his thoughts more in the last month. He had no way of determining whether that was a sign he should release the lines and sail from the safety of the marina, or just sell the *Horizon's Edge* to someone who would actually use her. Still, he could not seem to detach himself from the dream of adventure. He wasn't old. The machine-brain—his personal trainer—explained the concept of *real-age* to him. Based on his diet, body mass index, and other related wellness factors, his *real-age* was forty-five, but mentally, he felt ancient.

Ironically, Faith died shortly after declaring working with babies made her feel young again. The recurring thought passed into his mind: *Life is weird.* Speaking aloud to the empty cabin, "You'd laugh at that, wouldn't you, Faith?" He imagined her amused response and then realized he needed to gain control over his thoughts. There was no reason he should talk to himself and absolutely no reason he should anticipate Faith's responses. Emily had been correct, he wasn't moving on well or making progress in life. Faith's sudden death had left his heart wounded with a brutal scar that would not heal.

Despite Emily's absence since school started, he knew she loved him and also knew she was right—sailing might be the healing he needed, and every day at the dock was another day lost to grief. But the once-vibrant sunsets had lost their luster, the breeze no longer carried the promise of adventure and the gentle rocking of the boat only reminded him of the void.

The idea of facing the future without Faith crushed him. All this time and he still didn't know where to begin. Anger festered within him, directed at the unfairness. All he knew for certain was that he could not figure out how to plot a course in his despair. No matter the tide, the wind or the opportunity, Julian was as much tied up at the dock as his boat. The world seemed impossibly distant, a realm which he couldn't bring himself to explore. Grief held him back, keeping him from breaking free from the memories of Faith. Together their lives were entwined with the sea. What once carried them to new places, now only served as a painful reminder of his loss.

But the stages of grief Emily brought up would be the same anywhere. Denial was easy to overcome. Hearing your wife's body drop to the floor in the next room and having her die in your arms pushes a person through the reality of that stage quickly. Anger, however, became a lingering companion.

He had not prayed since Faith's memorial service, even his *Amen* on the deck had no divine target. It must have been obvious that he was questioning his faith. On that day, Emily gave him a book that explored the idea of deconstructing one's faith.

She said, "Here, Dad, I read this in college, and it really helped me make sense out of what I feel. Before mom died, I knew you wouldn't like what it says, but now I think it will help."

Julian read it in one sitting and wondered if he didn't agree. It seemed everyone was concluding church to be *non-essential*. The message of the book wasn't anything new. He started out life living and believing that way until, in his late twenties, he went through his very own deconstruction. Back then, he could have used the theme of the book, only in reverse. Nobody in his family would set foot in a church and they all believed in no God, no religion and no higher power. Atheism remained central to who he was, until he deconstructed—atheism. That was how he became a follower of Jesus. And now, a generation later, his daughter assumes that he should reverse course again. There was no question what he knew to be the truth—what he believed. Yet, in his heart, Julian felt a barrier, a sense of unworthiness that kept him from seeking solace in his chosen faith, in the comforting arms of the Prince of Peace.

He gave the book back to Emily and said, "Thanks. It was helpful. Reading that book made me realize what I need to do." She smiled, took the book back, and asked him, "What is it you need to do?"

"I stopped praying. When Mom died, I thought I lost my faith." Julian looked contemplative, and the wrinkles in his face softened. "I realize what I actually lost was my willingness to wrestle with God. Your book posed all the pertinent questions that I needed to contemplate. It made me realize the Bible is full of examples of men and women who asked those same questions and argued with God. Most of them worked through the problems in their lives while they questioned God's purpose and struggled with His Will. It didn't take long for me to realize I haven't lost my faith. I'm not questioning God's greatness after all, but I am figuring out my own weakness."

Chapter 4

THE SOUND OF HIS neighbor's radio spilled easily through the air, drifting over the cabins of a couple boats. It was far enough away that they didn't have to engage, yet close enough to break the silence. Julian's thoughts churned through the government's insidious weapons of control. While Julian had grown accustomed to the ever-watchful eyes of the advanced AI surveillance system, it was the human element—*the whisperers*—that truly baffled him. They were unpredictable and harder to safeguard against. How could a person set the blunt instrument of an authoritarian state against their neighbor?

Julian understood personal gain, buying influence, and even being true to ideology. None of those things escaped him, but ruining the life of someone who peacefully disagrees, seemed inhuman. With uneasiness still weighing on him, he renewed his commitment to be wary, even with his own neighbor, a man he had come to like.

Tom had become a part of the marina's community just a few weeks ago, his friendly and talkative nature quickly fit in with the liveaboards. That he shared in the collective loneliness of the community only added to his inclusion. Slightly older than Julian, and enjoying retirement on his boat, he made introductions quickly and engaged in the standoffish social life of Seattle's water people. He didn't inquire about personal things and never revealed too much either. But recently, his guarded behavior had slipped. Tom became open with his criticism of the *regime*. And even though what he said matched Julian's thoughts perfectly Julian countered with increased discretion. Wondering out loud about anything was an easy way to decrease your C3 score and often led to catastrophic outcomes.

"Hey, Julian!" Tom called out, waving from his boat. "How's it going?"

Julian forced a smile. "Hi, Tom. Not too bad. How about you?"

"Same old, same old," Tom replied with a shrug, his cheerful demeanor not faltering. He jumped onto the dock and made it halfway between them. "Julian, do you have a minute? I'm having a problem charting a course for my next voyage. Can I come over and talk it out with you? I'll bring the drinks."

Julian contorted his face in surprised acceptance. "I guess?" His response came out more as a question than an answer.

He had visited *Sapphire* twice. Once right after Tom arrived from cruising Alaskan waters, and the second time was a few days ago where they enjoyed coffee together while sitting on her deck. It takes little time for one sailor to evaluate another and Tom was the real thing. His Concordia yawl proved that—a stunning vessel. Even though the modest-sized sailboat had been constructed in the mid-1960s, the classic wooden boat's brightwork, meticulous paint and flawlessly rigged lines showed a nautical finesse that comes only with exceptional seamanship. Why Tom would need to ask Julian anything about sailing seemed suspicious. Julian was a competent sailor and had years of coastal sailing, but his blue-water experience was limited to a few training cruises for a celestial navigation certification. Helping Tom chart a course for his next voyage was unlikely.

"Wait there. I'll be over in a flash." Tom ducked out of view and returned carrying a colorful grocery bag. He walked up to the edge of the dock wearing a small backpack. "Permission to come aboard?"

Julian expected the self-invited guest would simply step onto his boat—that would be the norm. But Tom stood there almost at attention, and waited until Julian said, "Permission granted."

With an agile leap, Tom boarded the *Horizon's Edge*. He rummaged through his grocery bag, pausing briefly, before pulling out a beer and offering it to Julian. Tom's easy-going demeanor faltered, replaced by a sudden intensity as he spoke in a low, rumbling voice, revealing a depth of seriousness Julian hadn't seen before. "I've been needing to talk to you. Can we go below?"

Trust had become a luxury. Not the first time in history—the government turned people against each other, sowing seeds of doubt and mistrust. What only a couple of years ago was considered friendly banter between peers, had become a threat to a person's future. A series of verbal missteps months ago caused him tremendous grief. His C3 score dipped alarmingly following a conviction for what they labeled as *Offensive Speech—Public Health Threat*, a vague and broad charge. An anonymous source—*a whisperer*—turned Julian into the authorities and began the cascade of events which led to more and more problems. But the ridiculous aspect of the whole mess was the nature of the *Threat* that led to his conviction. He could not deny that he said, "The governor is a thug and all the politicians should be sent home," but the innocuous words resulted in criminal actions against him. And while the crime proved minor, it still broke through the guardrails of the First Amendment and crashed into the realm of *threatening the protected class of public servants charged with maintaining health and safety for all*.

Julian's C3 score was knocked down a level. The automated fine, euphemistically termed a *mandatory donation,* was deducted from his CBDC wallet. One thousand Central Bank Digital Currency dollars had been earmarked for the Revised Capital Adjustment fund and unceremoniously removed with the stated purpose of *ensuring equity*. However, like all the money the government managed for the people, it flowed into the morass of a bloated bureaucracy. The loss had been an annoyance rather than a hardship, but it prompted him to reevaluate his priorities and protect himself and those he cared about. Now, leading Tom down the companionway, he considered if he had actually learned anything about being cautious.

Without words, Tom gravitated to the settee and Julian took a seat at the dining table.

"You know, we might not have a choice with surveillance, but we can still choose who we trust," Tom said.

"Why should I trust you?"

Tom's eyes lit up with understanding. "You're right, Julian. Trust is scarce for a reason, but we don't have to let it define us. There's no reason for you to trust me yet, but give me some time, and I think you'll choose the red pill."

"It's a shame," Julian sighed. "I remember thinking *The Matrix* was the most brilliant science fiction movie ever. The pill choice is absolutely a classic. Sometimes, I feel like we are living it—in a simulation." He smirked. "Are you Morpheus, offering truth that will tear the fabric off a false reality? If so, you're wasting your time. I red-pilled a long time ago."

"If that's true, my job will be easy. I'm not speaking in code here. We both know we don't trust others. There are no omnipresent agents like in the movie, but whisperers are everywhere, even inside each of us. We simply require motivation whether it be a carrot or a stick—the best motivation is both. Create a reason to act, and we will turn in anyone." Tom managed an apologetic smile and continued with a challenge, "Do you know who turned you in?"

"What are you talking about?"

"You lost enough Community Contribution Credits to knock you down a level, you had to pay a thousand dollars in fines towards the Revised Capital Adjustment, plus some online re-education hours. It appears you also lost at least three friends." As Tom's expression turned serious, he leaned in. "It was a whisperer who reported you, Julian. Don't you wonder who would betray you like that?"

Julian stood up and backed away, "What the hell are you doing sitting in my boat talking to me like this? Get out!"

"Julian, please settle down. I'm on your side. I need to get under your skin to bring you up to speed faster. You don't need to trust me right now, but you do need to sit down. Now take a deep breath and I'll explain everything."

Julian's instincts kicked in. He snatched the beer bottle from the cup holder, gripping it tightly by its neck like a bat, his actions revealing a raw, unguarded side of him. But, before he could act on his threat to Tom, he saw the barrel of a gun pointed at his chest.

"Sit down," Tom said. "I'll explain everything, but first put down the beer bottle and give me your phone."

"You are in my boat, tossing around my personal information. You pull a gun on me, and I'm supposed to sit down and listen to you? What kind of idiot do you think I am?"

"You are not an idiot, but I am." He returned the gun to an inside waistband holster and covered the handle with his shirt. "Julian, I know far more about you than you can imagine. I need you to trust me. We have little time."

Chapter 5

"I WASN'T GOING TO hit you with the beer bottle. I just want you to leave."

Tom lowered his voice. "Trust me, Julian. No shooting. I reacted out of reflex, that's all. You'll soon see why I'm on edge. That is, if you'll give me time to explain."

"Do I have a choice? You've got fifty pounds on me and it looks like it's all muscle. Plus, you've got a gun. I guess if you were going to use it, I'd be bleeding out already. So, go ahead. I'm sitting. I'm not calmed down, but I'm listening."

Tom nodded, a somber expression on his face. "It's curious you would make that Morpheus remark. Is it because I'm black?" He pulled out a pair of sunglasses and put them on, staring at Julian with somber resolve. A few seconds ticked by before he stripped them off and laughed in a harmless chuckle ending in a disarming grin. "Neo was a hacker. He was onto the truth about the Matrix—he saw it when everyone else was blind. Julian, you have a lot in common with Neo. Sure, you're older, but you see patterns others don't. You understand we are all being played, lied to, kept in the dark and having our lives eroded. The dramatic among us say we are like frogs in a pot. The heat is turned up so slowly that by the time we realize we are being boiled, it's too late—we're too weak to jump out. If we were frogs, that might be how it works, but not as humans. Humans are special and we can believe we are boiling to death while bathing in tepid water. If we had the will, we can jump out anytime and save ourselves, but we don't—we comply. Much of what we value in life is already gone. Handed over without a fight. The consequences of resistance are terrifying. So we wait, remaining harmless as the imperial establishment divides and weakens us, manipulating our mindset to accept their control. Don't get me wrong, we are not cowards, we are simply wired to accept our plight and get along—even if it kills us."

Tom picked up his beer and took a long pull. "What do you think? Are we on the same wavelength?"

"I've not heard anybody talk like that—ever. But saying that now, is treason. Why would you say things like this? You know they listen. Phones, TVs, smart-house systems, drone bugs. AIs can even discern words through vibrations—windows, walls, even electric wiring. You're going to get us both arrested," Julian said.

Tom set his beer down. "I know you're not concerned about getting arrested and I know why. Do you remember when we met?"

"Who could forget it? I've never seen anybody make it into their slip under sail alone. That was the best boat handling I've ever seen. One man bringing a thirty-foot yawl into a marina in ten knots of wind. Incredible."

"I did that to get your attention."

"What do you mean?" Julian asked.

"As far as you know, I've never been on your boat before this. However, when I came to you in my scuba gear and asked if you would pay me to clean the bottom of your boat, I had ulterior motives. I don't need the money, but scraping a year's worth of sea life off your boat gave me a good excuse to check your boat for bugs and get close enough to assess your countermeasures. Your boat might have had a ton of crap needing to be scraped off, but your anti-surveillance methods are state-of-the-art.

"That's why you know as well as me, that nobody can monitor anything being said between us. Your countermeasures are not bad.

The state police or the feds would have to target you in order to monitor anything going on in here. In a way, I did you a favor and made sure there were no other surveillance devices on board or attached to your hull."

Julian rose from the table. This time he did it slowly with a pained look on his face. "So you have surveillance detection equipment that works underwater. And I thought I was paranoid. You are the crazy one. Actually, forget that. I'm still trying to figure out why you're here!"

"Alright, straight to the point," Tom said, taking a deep breath. He leaned back, looking relaxed but focused, hinting at the importance of what he was about to say. "I'm fighting the same fight you are. We are on the same side against this overreaching government. You are doing it by your forays into civil disobedience. Making sure they do not bug your conversations is only one thing you are up to. We know you've been finding connections between the University of Washington and the deep state, and you think you are helping the cause when you slow-walk a program or misdirect an agreeable AI. Your heart is in the right place, but in the grand scheme of things, you're wasting your time. They are letting you feel you're doing your part. It's like voting. You get to cast your vote to make you think you have agency. They allow you to feel good that you tried to change things, but in reality, they optimize for power, while the subjects of the realm are just trying to get by.

"We've watched you for a long time and decided the best place to approach you was here on your boat, so they assigned me to be here—for this day, for this conversation. In the game we're playing, timing is critical. You've been difficult to get to know. You're guarded and careful. I like that, but I cannot wait any longer because today is the day we have to talk."

Julian attempted to mirror Tom's relaxed demeanor, managing only to slow his breathing. He had resolved that, despite the presence of this rather intimidating man, the best course of action was to accept Tom's apology and chalk up the gun-brandishing to what Tom claimed were just reflexes. Still, Tom had not relinquished his insistence on being in control. The man had spied on him, weaseled his way on board, and confiscated his phone. He also sat between him and the companionway. Contradictions filled Julian's head—the guy seemed so friendly.

He decided to remain guarded, while accommodating his natural curiosity. "So, why approach me? If you're with the Feds, I get it — the old trick of targeting someone likely to break the law, lure them into a sting, and catch them red-handed. Classic FBI strategy. But I have no interest in helping you meet your quota of entrapping naive radicals."

"I'm not with the FBI or any government organization. My real name is Mitchell Thomas Cochrane—retired US Navy Captain. My friends call me Mitch. I'm sorry for the deceit, but if I'm caught doing this, my obituary will simply say I died of natural causes, my family will find it increasingly difficult to live a normal life and all my associates will be hunted down. As you can see, I must take my security seriously.

"I realized years back, I was unwittingly serving the wrong side. Naively, I believed I could make a difference just by sticking to my principles—the military encourages us to think that way. The problem is, there are so many layers, everyone can think they are staying true to their ethics while letting evil people pull the strings and ruin the world. As I began to age-out and it was time to retire, I gained a certain clarity about what was going on. The problem was not with the individuals—servicemen and women follow orders all the way up the chain of command. It is the true mission, the secret mission, orchestrated by the most despicable people the world has ever known, that is the problem. All military personnel are convinced the mission is to defend the Constitution and protect the people of the USA, but in reality, it is to serve those who benefit from the unique violence that comes from war power. Keep mayhem flowing, keep fear alive, and keep international balance about a quarter bubble off. That sums up the true mission, which has nothing to do with what any of us signed up for—we're just pawns.

"I finished my career, keeping my nose clean while I diagramed the intricacies of the power flow. The Pentagon proved to be the optimal location for my last several years of research. The Department of the Navy inadvertently helped me become an enemy of the state. I tell you all this only because I am a political fatalist, and I know I'm likely to end up in prison or dead.

"There are millions of us around the world. We don't carry cards and know only a handful of others, but association is not the point, and armed resistance would be foolish. Information is the key to winning this revolution, and the only weapon we need is truth. That is why we need you. Your skills can help us take down a special kind of evil that festers within the cabal of the powerful."

Julian was at a loss for words. The man's sincerity and passion were evident, yet Julian felt mentally overwhelmed and physically drained. Despite his desire to trust him, the idea seemed absurd. The notion of a man with such convictions incriminating himself was unthinkable, let alone a seasoned naval officer plotting treason. In this era, any whisperer could trigger the state's machinery, quickly ensnaring Tom, Mitch, or whoever he truly was. Julian's mind raced, *I could be the whisperer, the modern hero of a new world order. My C3 score would shoot up, Emily would be proud, and Asher's future more secure.*

He made a face, sarcasm suited him, but becoming a snitch never would. However, Julian could not help but suspect the man. Retired Captain Cochrane was likely an undercover agent stirring dissent, aiming to nab a would-be criminal. Firm in his conviction, Julian declared, "I don't believe you. You're lying about your name, who you are and you're setting me up—I won't fall for it."

"Look, I don't really care what you call me. I'd prefer Mitch. As for the trust issue—I don't blame you. The tactic of breeding distrust and then manipulating people to tell on each other for political, social and personal gain has been going on since the beginning of time. You're right, the FBI borrowed the tactic from the Stasi, and Homeland Security took it to new heights. Start with neighbors, friends and families. Turn children against their parents, wives against husbands and everyone against everyone else. Create a hierarchy of mistrust within education, the community, the workplace and the home." He lifted his hands outward. "You should see what's going on in the military."

Mitch let his hands drop to his lap. "This goes beyond the west coast, beyond the US—it's worldwide. The scale of what we're up against is immense, and it calls for a broader perspective. I've only been told what I need to know to deliver you, hopefully safely, to someone higher in the movement. Apparently you possess unique skills which set you apart. I know nothing more than that you are vital to what we're trying to achieve."

"Now I know you are kidding me. I'm decent with code, sure, but even around the University, I'm hardly indispensable. They keep me around because the AIs with hands and feet are too expensive to carry out the mundane tasks of plugging and unplugging wires. How could someone like me help in your grand scheme? I have nothing special to offer your revolution. You need to look for a better Neo. More likely, you need to find a more foolish would-be criminal," Julian said.

"I'm going to let you suspect me. That's fine. But you should know your actions—your quiet rebellion—up to this point, have been ineffectual. Nobody cares because it is of little consequence other than keeping you occupied until you retire or die. You can see it, there are fewer and fewer people in this world who will fight for freedom. Currently, it's a war of attrition. Most people are content just being looked after, trusting that a powerful government will lead them to a brighter future. But at what cost?

"Freedom is virtually gone, individuality is struggling for air and the concept of liberty is too confusing for lazy brains. The allure of a global government is seductive and men like you and me are in the way of that progress. We are the last line of defense of liberty, yet we are old. They want us to be dead, but will be content if we are weak and tired. They know they are close to realizing the new utopian world of their collectivist dreams and we are the problem." Mitch took up his beer bottle and leaned forward. "The way I see it, they are partly correct, and that's what keeps me going. As long as we are the problem, we can offer hope to the people." Mitch extended his hand and recoiled it as if to emphasize a thought. "What do you know about warfare?"

"Nothing," Julian admitted.

"Does this sound familiar to you? *We mutually pledge to each other our lives, our fortunes, and our sacred honor.*"

"Yeah, isn't that from the Revolutionary War?"

"The Declaration of Independence, adopted by the Continental Congress on July 4, 1776. We find ourselves at the same juncture. It's too late to put our trust into the classical liberal methods of the Enlightenment. Those avenues have been co-opted. It's also too late for lies—even lies for noble purposes. I am who I say I am. We are in a hell of a battle, and we need all the help we can get. *Vive Libere Aut Mori*, or if you prefer it in English: Live Free or Die. The choice is yours. You can be obedient to the congenial tyrants, forcing you to live the way they see fit, or you can fight for freedom."

"This feels like a setup, or maybe you've lost your mind. Either way, this conversation ends now. It's time for you to leave. I never want to see you again. Even if any of this is true, I cannot possibly be any help to the cause of freedom. My life might not be ideal, but I will not be locked up for some stupid cause dreamed up by a bunch of old patriots," Julian said.

"I'm not leaving. Whether or not you join us, I need you to hear me out. There's more at stake here than you realize. Weigh my words and then make your decision. There is more you need to learn, and they will give you time to think it through. One consideration is your daughter Emily, another is your grandson Asher. Their freedoms are almost gone, and they cannot see it. Most people are blind, but you are not. And once you see what is happening, it's impossible to unsee. You lost Faith because her work compelled her to obey the vaccine mandates. Julian, we all have skin in the game, whether or not we think we are playing."

Chapter 6

JULIAN PACED OVER TO the galley. His gaze lingered on a knife resting on the cutting board. For a fleeting moment, the absurd idea of wielding it to drive Mitch from his boat crossed his mind, a testament to the brewing desperation within him. But it wasn't the equalizer he needed and he had questions which required an answer. "What do you know about my family? You're sitting here on my boat, you've pointed a gun at me, and you keep talking like a criminal. Now, you're bringing my family into it. You've got a hell of a way to convince me we are on the same side!"

"Listen, if it were up to me, I'd spend the next month slowly bringing you up to speed. We are on the same side—you just don't have the information that will persuade you. I promise if you spend the next twenty-four hours with me and a few of my friends, you will fully understand the extent of what we're facing. Tomorrow, you'll be free to go along your own path. If you decide to turn me in and expose the plans we reveal to you, then I won't be the one to stop you. I've been one step ahead, looking over my shoulder for too long. If this operation doesn't work, I might welcome an end to the struggle."

"So you're kidnapping me, and then you're just going to let me go?"

"Julian, you're being overly dramatic. Let's spend the next hour getting *Horizons Edge* ready to sail. Her hull is clean, it's a beautiful

Autumn day, and the wind will show up before long. We can have a leisurely sail and get to know each other better before rendezvousing with a woman you need to meet."

"Oh, this is rich. So you are not only kidnapping me, but you're going to force me to break the law and leave the dock without documentation to meet some mysterious revolutionary."

Mitch's tone was casual, almost reassuring. "You won't be breaking any laws—today, at least. Look at this," Mitch said, displaying his phone. "Seems you applied for a recreational permit yesterday. Surprise—it's already approved. We are free to enjoy a couple days of sailing. Here is another bit of drama for you." Mitch slid his legs to the side of the bench and placed an elbow on one knee. "Your actions, until now, have been resistance. Those small acts of defiance, they count, but unchecking a box that should be checked, taking a processor offline for repairs when you know it's just fine, purposefully inserting a code loop that looks like it was just a mistake, are not creating the change we need. That has been your attempt at resistance, and I applaud you. It's not nothing, but you will find my friends and I are not content with being a fly in the ointment. We're in a deeper fight. We're combatants in a larger battle, and we need you to elevate your role. Julian, we need you to join us where the stakes are higher."

Chapter 7

"THAT SMILE ON YOUR face says it all," Mitch yelled over the noise created by the wind filling the sails and water spilling around the hull as they healed northward on a port tack.

From the helm, Julian shouted back, "Maybe that's because all I have to do is jibe, and your sorry ass will be in the water." He turned the wheel to the right, but only enough to give the Point-No-Point light a wide berth. "Were you born on a sailboat, or does the Navy insist all their officers are expert sail handlers?"

Mitch worked his way back to the safety of the cockpit. He pulled off his hood and settled into the protection of the downwind bench seat. "There was no sailing in Compton. It was a rough neighborhood, and I spent my formative years running for my life. But a funny thing happened as I got bigger—I stopped running away from getting beat up and started running for the track team. I excelled in high school and got accepted into the Naval Academy. As a plebe, I fell in love with sailing, and my track coach reluctantly allowed me to take part on the sailing team as long as it didn't interfere with any track and field commitments.

"Annapolis is a wonderful environment for sailing, and, by my junior year, I was headed for Olympic qualifiers. It's how I learned about optics. You're going to love this! Remember, it was the early eighties, *Sailing World* published an article with a picture showing me wearing white shorts and a white polo shirt. You might ignore the stark contrast in the team photo, so the adjoining article referred to me as the collegiate sailor who…" He held up air quotes. "…*is a reminder of the myriad shades of existence that contribute to the kaleidoscope of our shared humanity.*" Mitch laughed. "I went to track practice, and the coach said, 'You're off the team. From now on, you'll be working out at the marina with the lighter shades of humanity.'"

"So, did you go to the Olympics?" Julian asked.

"Nope. I found myself aboard the *USS Kitty Hawk* during the '84 Summer Games, watching my Olympic dreams sail away without me. Never raced again after that."

"So if we're not going to kill each other, why won't you tell me where we're going or who we're meeting?"

"I like that, Julian. Right to the point. And you're right, I can't kill you, even if I wanted to." He faked a villainous grin. "To tell you the truth, I don't know how they've pegged you as—*the one*. However, I know who you're meeting. It is kind of like *The Matrix*. You're going to meet the Oracle. Okay, not really, but she is very smart and very well placed to make incredible change. In some sense, she will determine your destiny, but without a doubt, she is not the Oracle. Then again, you're not exactly Keanu Reeves either. Or are you?"

Mitch didn't wait for an answer. "I don't know why the lady pulled me off a critical job, only to have me watch, capture, and babysit you. I mean, you seem like a nice guy and all. I'm sure you can hold your own around tech conversations, but truthfully, I don't see anywhere in your file where you are the *top dog*. Sorry to say, not even in your own department at the U-dub." Mitch sat back and motioned outward with his right hand. "Why don't you tell me why they want you, and I'll tell you who wants you."

"I'm as clueless as you. During Y2K, the University recruited me for my expertise in programming, but to tell you the truth, my career has been winding down a little each year since then. I'm basically the cable guy in the computer science department. They won't even notice that I'm gone when I retire—or go missing." Julian laughed as if a switch had flipped. He trusted Mitch. His gut told him to, but his mind remained vigilant. It was an internal conflict he could live with, and being on the water helped him look at things more philosophically.

"Great. I'm risking my life for an obsolete geek. Well, it won't matter much if I tell you now anyhow. We rendezvous with another boat in less than an hour, where you'll meet one of the leaders in the war against insanity. Her name is Anastasiya Valentina Volkov. She's commonly known as Val. Have you ever heard of her?"

"Can't say that I have," Julian admitted.

"You might have crossed paths with her story without knowing it, felt her influence, even if the flashy world of socialites and jet-setters seems far from your own life. To say she is a public figure is an understatement—Val is an icon. Her career began as a model and turned to acting. She's Russian, from Donbas. After she dominated the silver screen in Eastern Europe, she set to work on the rest of the world. One of her notable accomplishments is the vast number of audiences she appeals to. Not only is she beautiful, but she's fluent in seven or eight languages, making for a truly international career. Just wait till you meet her. Val's a force of nature with a style that's hard to ignore. She leaves an impression, whether or not you're ready for it."

Mitch pulled Julian's phone out of his pocket and handed it to him. "Your daughter. Put her on speaker and tell her the truth. We are sailing, but leave out the whole kidnapping thing, and say nothing you'll regret. I'm trusting you," Mitch said with all seriousness.

Emily's voice trembled, "Dad, I'm scared. I came home from work today, and everything is gone. I mean, not everything, but all of Jonathan's things. He never called, and there's no note. The neighbor said she saw him get in a black SUV with two women, and a van came right after and carried some things out. He was supposed to pick Asher up from school. They called me when he was late and I raced to get Asher. What should I do?"

"I don't know what to say. Is Asher alright?"

"Yes. Why wouldn't he be?"

"Honey, hold on a minute. I'll be right back."

Julian put his phone on mute and locked eyes with Mitch. "Do you have anything to do with this?"

"Not me. But it's possible Val did. The report I was given about your family indicated him as an ongoing problem."

"Wait a minute—Jonathan? But why would someone like Val take an interest in him?" Julian asked.

"Remember, when I asked if you wanted to know who turned you in? Who the whisperer was?"

"What! You actually knew?"

Mitch looked somber and said, "You must have suspected it was Jonathan. His C3 score went up around the same time, and he fell deeper into his gaming addiction."

"No, I didn't notice..." Julian's voice trailed off.

Mitch pulled off his sunglasses and pointed to the phone in Julian's hand. "It might take more than a minute."

"I'm back," Julian said into the phone. "Emily, can you sit tight for a little longer? I've got some connections that might help figure out what happened to Jonathan. I'll call you when I find something."

"We're not going anywhere," she said. "Dad, are you sailing?"

He looked at Mitch, who seemed curious about what Julian would say. "I decided since you and Asher have been too busy to go out with me, that I'd take my new friend Tom out for a sail. He's the one that owns *Sapphire*, that beautiful wooden boat I told you about."

"I better go and see what I can dig up about Jonathan. I love you." Julian ended the call.

Mitch reached for the phone, and Julian handed it back without hesitation. "You are a cautious sort. Nice breadcrumb giving up *Sapphire* like that. Hedging your bets, just in case you don't make it back?"

"Hey, I didn't come right out and tell her the truth about you kidnapping me."

"It's okay. I would have done the same thing. But look, I don't know if Val is involved in what happened to Jonathan. It wouldn't surprise me. Val's team expressed concern about your daughters boyfriend. They uncovered that Jonathan turned you in—again. He filed a report on the *Anonymous Tip Hotline*, claiming to have serious evidence against you.

"I admire how careful you are about your security, but they believe Jonathan has been recording Emily's conversations with you. It appears you have said some things against the state, and they will convict you, this time not being so gentle."

"That's insane! I have said nothing. No threats, nothing criminal...." The confidence bled out of his voice. "Just my opinions. The only thing I do is question the overreach of the government into everybody's lives. That can't be a crime."

"It is, if they choose to prosecute. Washington, Oregon and California have the highest rates of prosecutions of domestic terrorists. They only care about your opinion when it's the wrong opinion. The conviction rate is high, though they will allow a plea bargain if you agree to pay fines, turn against others and publicly reverse your statements."

"That's bullshit! I'm not a terrorist!"

"Not yet, but you will be, eventually. I'm betting on sooner rather than later. If you join us, at least your crimes will count for something." Mitch breathed in deeply and scanned the water, then spoke in a slow, calm voice, "Julian, if you join us, you will be with people who can help you and your family through what's coming. The idea of an individual being free to choose their life and live their dreams has been lost. Shaping your own destiny, if it was ever a thing, is long gone. Our generation is not the last one that cares, but it is the last that remembers how it was. Evil has been normalized and obedience sanctified."

"You know, that's all just perfect. Your rhetoric fits so nicely into my views. If I was a moron, I'd grab onto your life ring of hope. We can sit around the campfire and chant all those patriotic mantras—'Freedom is not free,' 'United we stand, divided we fall,' and your favorite—'Live free or die.' They've all spun around in my head, but they mean nothing without action." Julian's face flushed with anguish, he slumped into the helm seat and tried to slow his breathing. "I need to know my daughter and grandson are not in any danger. I don't care about Jonathan, but if I knew what happened to him, that he had not been harmed, I would feel better about what we are doing here," Julian said.

"Why don't you steer us back on course, and I'll reach out and see what happened to him. I assure you, nobody is going to hurt Emily or Asher. Val does not operate that way."

"I want to believe you, I really do. But why would she take Jonathan?"

"You don't see it, do you? Val needs you. I'm only here because of that. I've got a few allies working with me, but Val? She's got an entire network, hundreds of people, totally dedicated to this cause. The *why* is beyond me, but you're the one they've singled out. My job is to bring you to her. But I'd guess Jonathan's actions threatened to derail her operation. Val's making sure she keeps you out of trouble. Just so you're aware, she has top-notch security. They'll erase any compromising data and move Jonathan somewhere he can't cause harm. If the authorities can't find him and his evidence against you, they won't have a reason to search for you."

Julian stood, his back straight and both hands on the wheel. Mitch was right, it was time for a change in course. "Okay, you make your calls and get me the information I need. In the meantime, I better point us away from danger. I've steered clear of the rocks all my sailing life, both literal and metaphorical. Today's no day to change that habit." He spun the wheel hard to the right and caught Mitch off guard, causing him to grab a handhold. Julian looked at him with a sly grin that betrayed no guilt. "Sorry. Did I forget to say, *coming about*?"

Unperturbed by the sudden course change, Mitch deftly adjusted the sails, his hands moving with the ease of long-practiced skill. He seemed to enjoy the warm sun that bathed the deck as much as the increased speed of the new tack. "I've gotten to know Val pretty well in the last couple of years, and you should understand she appreciates family and will protect yours. Even if that means sidelining your daughter's opportunistic boyfriend. You know, Jonathan gets a D+ as a father figure to Asher. Do you know who the biological father is?"

"Emily never shared that kind of thing with me. Faith knew, but I guess she figured it was not important. I get the feeling that you like to pry where you have no business. You knew about Emily and Asher, and you looked into the cause of Faith's death."

"Information is my job. It's how we stay out of prison, and sometimes, it keeps us alive. You'll see. Let's stay on this course while I check on a few things for you."

Chapter 8

"WHY WOULD JONATHAN AGREE to leave Emily and Asher behind and fly back to his mom's place in Las Vegas? That just makes no sense."

"Actually, it does. He's being supported by a woman with a job who has a kid. His only responsibility is to pick the kid up at school and walk him home and even then, he doesn't engage with Asher. The rest of the time he's gaming. Val's security team said it thrilled him when they showed up. Their job was to act like they were continuing the investigation, and he eagerly gave them the recordings that incriminated you in exchange for a thousand gaming tokens. When they offered to send him out of state *for his own protection*, he couldn't wait to jump on a flight home to his mommy," Mitch chuckled.

"You should call Emily and break the news. Jonathan surrendered his phone to Val's agent, but she should be able to call his mother and talk to him, or wait a couple of hours, until his replacement phone is set up." Mitch took on a serious expression. "Julian, it's important you keep the charade going. Jonathan thinks he's a hero of the state, and he's being treated as special for his brave efforts of turning you in. From the looks of it, he wants nothing to do with Emily or Asher. Otherwise, he wouldn't have recorded her phone calls and thrown her father under the bus."

"Actually, I'm just going to text her."

Mitch pulled out the phone and said, "Good idea. What do you want me to tell her?"

Julian didn't argue and dictated, "*Jonathan is fine. Lost his phone. Had to go to his mother's. Call her in a couple hours. Something to do with Homeland Security.* And insert a *telephone emoji*—that way she will know I'm trying hard to communicate."

As the phone slid back into his pocket, Mitch said, "I'm sorry for all this. I know this day is not going like you planned, but it will all make more sense soon enough."

"Thanks for the info, but I can't quite wrap my head around why some lady-mastermind would want to meet with me," Julian remarked with a hint of suspicion. Then, as if distracted, he checked their course on the compass and peered around the foresail. "We're heading straight for the shipping lanes, right where they cross into Canadian waters. The winds have dropped off. At this speed, we'll be navigating the Strait of Juan de Fuca in the dark. Are we headed to Victoria?"

"Nope." Mitch glanced at his watch, his eyes grim. "Actually, in exactly eight minutes and twenty-five seconds, you'll be leaving this boat. Timing is crucial here."

"What are you talking about?"

"Here's the deal. You are out for a sail with a friend. Within forty-four hours, you are scheduled to return to your slip. Your boat will return, and a white guy wearing your cap and clothes will tie up and they will see your black friend heading back to his yawl. Nobody will suspect anything unusual. However, in a few minutes, you'll prepare to board Val's yacht, and then you will learn all the things that I can't tell you or don't know." Mitch raised his eyebrows and produced a confident smile. "Check your chart plotter for a vessel about to intersect us."

After a fleeting glance at the plotter, Julian angled his body to scan around the genoa, towards Port Townsend. His eyes bulged when he saw the prow of a huge yacht heading in their direction. "Is that

Val's boat? The plotter says they're going to cross our wake in about fifteen minutes."

"Well then, that means you'll only be cold for a short while. Fortunately, you have just enough time to get into your drysuit."

"I don't have a drysuit."

"When you were at the gym this morning, I stowed one." Mitch stood up, released the clasps, lifted the hinged seat-top and pulled out an all-black, one-piece drysuit. He walked over to Julian and said, "I'll take the helm. You should hurry." He looked at his watch and back at the megayacht. "Yeah, they're right on time." Gesturing to the drysuit, he sighed, "That thing won't put itself on. You are leaving this boat at the designated minute, so I suggest you kick off your boat shoes and climb in. It's your best chance for surviving the plunge. You'll want to give me a chance to check the seal around your wrists and neck, or you will be shivering your way to hypothermia."

"You're telling me I have to jump into the water?" Julian's voice rose in disbelief, a mixture of fear and incredulity.

"I can't wait to find out why Val wants your brain. Can't say I've seen anything worthy of a revolution, but it takes all kinds. People who are trying to avoid being executed as traitors tend not to want to attract the attention of the authorities. So you will leave *Horizon's Edge* and get scooped up a few minutes later by *Elysium Prime*."

"I'm supposed to believe she doesn't want to attract attention, yet the AIS says the *Elysium Prime* is a two hundred foot vessel." Skepticism oozed from Julian's tone, "Sure—that won't attract any attention."

If Mitch noticed Julian's sarcasm, he gave no indication. Yet he methodically tightened the zip closure of the drysuit and ensured every seal was secure. He pulled the hood over Julian's head, adjusting the Velcro around his neck with a firm tug and took on a mission-ready appearance that commanded attention. "The hull of the boat will look like it's going to plow right into you." Mitch held a firm hand on each of Julian's shoulders and stared directly into his eyes. "Listen carefully. I will not repeat this. When you see the steel of the hull pass, you need to tread water like your life depends on it. Clasp your wrist as tight as you can and hold your arms up over your head. Look into the eyes of the guy hanging from the davit just above the waterline. He's got forearms like Popeye, and if you're not kicking enough to get yourself half out of the water when he comes flying by, he'll dislocate your shoulders. *Kick to un-stick.* Got it?"

"This is insane!" Julian yelled.

In a decisive, almost reflexive motion, Mitch gripped Julian firmly and guided him with an unexpected strength to the edge of the boat. With a calculated push, he propelled Julian overboard, plunging him into the cold embrace of the sea.

Chapter 9

HE LONGED FOR SOMETHING familiar to anchor him. The shower was somewhat refreshing, but the lingering saltwater in his ears only amplified his sense of disorientation. They had given him jeans—a subtle reminder of his age with their relaxed fit—and yet a perfect match for his unchanged 33-inch inseam from his college days. Julian was fit, successfully staving off a beer belly, though his washboard abs were now only a memory. He tucked his aqua-green *Elysium Prime* polo shirt into the jeans. Although he wasn't keen on the belt with its loud nautical flags, it was a necessity to keep his pants up over his narrow hips. Slipping his feet into a brand-new pair of flip-flops, he was startled by a knock at the door.

Greeting him was a youthful man, probably in his twenties, flashing a bright-white smile. His attire matched Julian's, complete with an *Elysium Prime* polo and a garish belt, suggesting it was the crew's standard uniform. His khaki capri pants and pristine white boat shoes differed, making Julian appreciate his own comfortable jeans and modest footwear. "Hi, I'm Cedric. Pleasure to meet you, Julian. I've been sent to escort you. Have you met Val before?" His accent carried a hint of Croatia, evoking memories of Julian's past travels.

"No. Can't say that I've ever heard of her before today."

Cedric laughed out loud, only to contort his face in disbelief when he realized Julian was not joking. "Very well." He smiled as he turned around. "Follow me. Your life will never be the same. Don't worry, she doesn't bite—strangers, that is." This time, he didn't curtail his laughter.

The opulence of the salon challenged Julian's assumptions about being on the water. Its spacious layout, panoramic windows and plush seating appeared incongruous with sea travel, yet he gazed out at the familiar breathtaking views. To the east, the snow-capped North Cascades stood tall, while cobalt blue waters lapped gently at Whidbey Island's shoreline, not too far away. White owned the ships interior, but crisp aqua-green lines traveled throughout the decor, successfully adding a captivating visual effect. An interior wall held enormous portraits of a striking model. They appeared to be a study in aging, but Julian's attention was diverted by the sound of a piano.

As he moved through the yacht, the music guided him around a corner. A woman sat at a grand piano, her back to him. She had brown hair with golden highlights that fell in waves down her back. Broad shoulders, a slender waist, and she wore a sleeveless dress.

Julian remained still, watching the woman play from memory. The song, "Dreams" by Fleetwood Mac, drew him in. Each deliberate note formed the familiar conclusion and then she lowered her head and withdrew her hands away from the keys. He wondered, *should I clap?* When she turned to him, he realized he had made the right decision to remain quiet. Tears traced her high cheekbones; she quickly wiped them away, looking embarrassed. Then, her face brightened with a perfect smile as she walked confidently towards Julian. She was barefoot, her teal silk dress stopping at the calf, her pearl earrings and delicate silver necklace added a sense of elegance.

"Julian, I'm glad to have you on board. I'm Val, and this is the *Elysium Prime*, my home. I hope you will be comfortable here."

He struggled to remember Val's full name, the one Mitch had mentioned just an hour earlier—*Anastasiya Val*—but he could not recall the rest of the foreign sounds. Her accent was subtle, almost as though she had spent years in America but retained a hint of her origins.

"Thank you so much for dropping in. We have so much to talk about in so little time. I am at an unusual advantage—uncommon, anyway. I know all about you, and you know nothing about me." Slowing just before she reached Julian, she positioned her feet in a manner reminding him of a woman preparing to accept a formal dance. Her fingertips lightly grazed his forearms and signaled that their greeting would be old-world chic. She leaned in to place a delicate kiss on his cheek, expressing her warm regard, and he received it as if it were a greeting he encountered frequently. Releasing her light grasp, she spun around and led him to an enormous u-shaped couch. Her dress rippled and fluttered with her light steps, and a short slit freed her legs below her knees as she sat and crossed her feet at the ankles.

"Did your wife know?" Val asked.

"Know what?"

"Know about your criminal record."

"I don't have a criminal record," Julian said.

"No, no, no. I do not mean it as an insult, and I am not questioning the depths of your relationship with your wife. May I say, I am so sorry she is no longer with us. I'm sure it is difficult to move on without her. So sudden. Tragic even."

While Julian typically appreciated candor, at this moment he felt like he should sprint through the doors, jump into the water and take his chances swimming to shore, yet her eyes captured his thoughts as much as her words.

"Julian, you are one of us. You subscribe to liberty. Not as a selfish act, but as the natural law in which all humanity deserves to be born into. You have wanted that freedom since your first offense against your government—your first hack. You were what, fourteen? Amazingly, you didn't get caught for three years—brilliant! But after the arrest, the only conviction they could get was a misdemeanor.

However, they did manage to banish you from using any computers and sealed your records. After your juvenile probation ended at eighteen, they expunged you of any criminal wrongdoing, and as far as the world was concerned, you got a second chance. College—computer science major—a bold move on your part, and then you lived a normal life as another brick in the wall. Or did you?"

His voice held a mix of resignation and defiance. "How you unearthed that history is beyond me. But dredging up my past? It won't intimidate me now," Julian said.

"Oh, Julian, I have no interest in blackmail, if that's what you're getting at. I'm not looking for mercenaries either—I have plenty of those. If you are a genuine believer in the cause of freedom, then you are on the right boat. If not, I only ask that you go away for a few weeks. I have a lovely place in the Philippines. It's primitive and there's no connection to the outside world. But it has everything else, including a cook, and the small staff would be available to you. Think of this as a job interview. One where you win whether you take the offer or not.

"If you take it, you will be an active member of the opposition to the corrupt orthodoxy that is ubiquitous throughout the world. You will be a traitor—a traitor to a government unworthy of its people. However, if at the end of this interview, you do not accept my offer, I would be disappointed, but you would be safe. You have done nothing to deserve retribution. Frankly, you know too much, even now, for me to allow you to go back to your regular life. However, in a few weeks, I'll either be crossing the Pacific in glory, or I'll be dead."

"So, you are leading a war against the United States from this ship and you want me to join in. That is the most absurd thing I've ever heard. I'll take the free vacation," Julian said.

"Not that kind of war. I'll be as transparent as possible. I'm asking you to allow me the time I need to explain what our movement is about and where you fit in. You will see we are not waging war against the United States. Your country is wonderful, and we all should emulate your core values. Our enemies, however, are those who wield power against the people, and they are quite international.

"Our tactics are simple. We expose the truth, since lies always oppress people." She hesitated, pressed her lips together in thought, and then smiled as she said, "Our motto should be, 'The truth will set you free.' Our battle is against the influential few who govern with deception—our strength emerges by unveiling the truth."

Chapter 10

Rising gracefully from the couch, Val moved toward the wall adorned with stunning oversized photographs. Suddenly, Julian now remembered what Mitch had told him about the Russian model turned actress—her full name—Anastasiya Valentina Volkov. Four photographs were hung in order, each a model's pose of Val, showcasing her from a young girl to nearly her present age. Each image was a piece of art, capturing the progression of her stunning beauty.

On the wall, an empty space was reserved for one more photograph. Val, standing by the image at the far left, extended a meaningful gesture towards it—a quiet yet persuasive prompt for insightful reflection.

"What do you see?"

Julian stood at a distance that was best for viewing and stared into the penetrating eyes of the teenaged girl. They were brilliant blue, and her dark brown hair fell around her face radiating hopefulness. Her lips were full, like most young girls, but they looked chapped under a veil of lipstick. There was no other evidence of makeup. Her cheeks had a natural blush, a rose backdrop for translucent freckles scattered on each side of her nose. She wore a white peasant blouse with a drawstring neckline which accentuated her collarbones and added to the impression that she was underfed. He saw all these things but would not say them. "I imagine that is you, as a teenager."

It surprised him to hear the laugh that came from deep inside her. With a fluid motion, Val straightened and moved towards Julian. She grasped his arm, her touch light yet conveying a need for support, steadying herself from an invisible fall. Her hand was so warm and her grip so soft—he moved away suddenly, feeling awkward.

"Seriously, you American men communicate so much through understatement." She went back to the photograph as if she were highlighting it for an auctioneer. "This is the earliest picture I have of myself. A talent scout for the Communist Party of the Soviet Union took it. He raped me that day."

She moved back to her place on the couch and sat on the edge. "Julian, please sit down." Her face became apologetic, accepting his shock. "It's long in the past, and I dealt with it."

"Why are you telling me this?"

"Darling, it's my job to recruit you to our cause and put you to work. Normally, I buy people, make them an offer they cannot refuse. But, from everything I know about you, that is not an option since you are already rich. So, we should become friends and build our relationship on trust. Since a person cannot trust someone they do not know, I must share my story with you." A steward arrived with an elegant rolling cart filled with appetizers and a variety of drinks. "You must be hungry after your swim. Was it dreadfully cold?" She poured a small amount of brandy into a huge goblet and handed it to him.

"I was fourteen years old. A mining accident the year before had taken my father's life. Each year, someone would set up an audition for all the girls. It was glamorous! We all wanted to be chosen. The girls lined up, and a man would walk along the rows, pinch our chins, and tell some of us to spin around. If he liked what he saw, he told his beautiful assistant to set up a time for the next day. She handed me a flier explaining the opportunity. I was to show up the next evening wearing my very best clothes. He would take some preliminary photographs and then return to Moscow. After a few months, lucky girls around the country would serve the USSR with their Soviet good looks.

"I went at the scheduled time, and he offered me a Coke, my first ever. It tasted strange, but of course, it would, so I drank all of it. He had me pose. I imagined I was a movie star. The next thing I knew, I woke up with the photographer on top of me, barely able to breathe. I realized he had drugged me and I tried to scream. He woke up and covered my mouth, and spouted some nonsense about beauty, responsibility, and advancing my career. I was naive and scared and didn't know that the promises of fame were empty. No photos or telegrams ever came. The next year, a different glamour scout for the USSR showed up, and I kept my distance."

"I thought you said you got even," he said, immediately regretting his words. An intensity seemed to build from deep inside her as she responded with measured control.

"I said I dealt with it. When I was sixteen, I killed him."

Julian held his breath, waiting for Val to continue, until awareness took hold and he resumed shallow breaths to not be too obvious. Eventually, she appeared satisfied with Julian's response and continued her story.

"Two years later, the same photographer returned. I saw him enter a restaurant with a woman. Dressed for a night out, I approached him and whispered a bold suggestion for a nude photoshoot. My touch on his thigh left an unmistakable invitation. His companion didn't seem to care; in fact, you might say she seemed amused as he instructed me to meet him discreetly in his room.

He offered me a Coca-Cola. I pretended to drink and played my part, feigning various emotions and then passing out. Act two was an indifferent performance—I felt nothing. This time, as he fell asleep, I left him to his dark dreams and returned with my straight razor. A person develops certain skills growing up on a collective farm, and I sliced his neck from carotid to carotid, straight through his trachea."

"Two weeks later, a letter came with this photo of me, found among the deceased photographer's effects. Even though the photo was two years old, the letter came with official instructions. I left my vital role as a farm laborer, took the trains to Moscow and joined the Soviet equivalent of a modeling agency."

Val relaxed her jaw and motioned towards the food cart. "You haven't eaten a thing, would you care for some crackers and cheese? Here let me serve you. Caviar Blinis—miniature buckwheat blini, topped with crème fraîche and caviar." She sprinkled a garnish of finely diced red onions and chives across the plate and handed it to him. "More brandy?"

"There is no way I could eat after a story like that. It will take me a while to recover. You're right though. I'm not motivated by money. But, if you're trying to build trust, a story like that is probably not the best way to go about it." Despite Julian's attempt at humor, he couldn't match his host and relax back into the plush couch. "You said I'm rich. Why would you say that? I've been at the university for twenty-five years—you probably know how much I make—it's not like I'm a football coach. And Faith made more money per hour than I did, mostly working part time. Still, nobody ever got rich with our wages, especially not living in the city with a kid."

"Did you ever tell her about your investment?" Val asked.

"What are you talking about?"

"Really. You never told her!?" she smirked.

Julian held out his hands and shrugged his shoulders, "I don't know what you are talking about."

"Ah, I see why this is confusing to you."

From the couch she pointed to the second picture. "What do you see?"

This photo showed a more mature Val in her early twenties. She stood alone and her figure cast a stark contrast against the abstract backdrop. The muted colors added a sense of reflection and somber contemplation. But something in her eyes confirmed an inner strength and betrayed her solemn expression. "I would say things are bleak and you didn't want to get your photo taken."

She pulled a small pillow to her chest, crossed her arms over it and tucked her feet up under her. "I was nineteen. They had assigned me a leading role in a motion picture and took the photo the day after my sterilization. I left the hospital in the night, and they flew me to Moscow. My career was certain, I was to become a Mosfilm icon, and they would take no chances. Of course, I had no say in the matter, but probably would have agreed to the sensibility of ensuring my girlish figure—I would do anything for the Party. So, you are correct, it was bleak. In Russia, we understand life is difficult—even tragic. When they confirmed my status as a film star, it was not surprising that it would be with blood." She relaxed the pillow and returned her bare feet to the floor.

"Marriage would come and the studio would decide when and to whom. But lovers? That was up to me. Of course my life was highly curated, and the news and intrigue regarding it, even more so. The slanted edge, that space between the movie scripts and my scripted life, narrowed. Leading men naturally became my male companions on the set and off. We would drink and share intimate secrets as if we were free to explore the depths of romance. But there was always something I would hold back. We all have our secrets, and each of us has our reasons for keeping things from those we love."

"Maybe I'm missing something here," Julian said. "These days, it feels like the entire world is in a hurry to leave me behind. My daughter thinks I'm walking a tightrope between losing my mind in grief and being uncaring. The wives of my buddies can't decide if I'm just really down or actually toxic. Either way, those rare check-ins are even rarer now. I appreciate it—hanging out with someone who has checked out is a downer for those trying to fit in. But now, you've thrown me into your world and it's like I'm the one who's normal. You and Mitch make me look like the definition of normalcy. And what makes it worse, is that I can't even figure out what you want from me. Could you at least tell me that?"

"Your skills, of course. I need you to know it is not the time for secrets. I no longer have the luxury or desire to hide things from those I wish to be close to, and I expect—reciprocation."

A moment passed. Julian felt uneasy, but he stayed silent, still wondering why he was on this yacht, with this woman.

Val sipped her brandy and set it down, her eyes lingering on Julian as if measuring his readiness. Rising gracefully, she seemed to almost float towards the third photo. As her back blocked his view, Julian realized he couldn't recall the details of this image, only that it featured Val. Then, with a slow turn, she unveiled the third scene. Compelled by curiosity, Julian stood and moved closer.

At first glance, the photograph seemed to be taken in a studio against muslin curtains under intense light. But a closer look revealed a different truth. The background was a crowd of robed men standing in the harsh Middle Eastern sun, creating an illusion with their backs.

A younger Val stood in a sliver of shadow, dressed in a tan blouse with an unbuttoned collar and epaulets. She resembled a character from "Casablanca" with her rakish smile and shirt tucked into slacks, accentuating her slim waist. The shadow cast her in grays, highlighting a study in contrast.

Despite Val's captivating eyes and confident demeanor, it wasn't her that dominated the scene. In her hands, she loosely held the hilt of a sword, its gleaming blade prominent in the bright foreground. The point disappeared off the frame, while the ornate handle, adorned with mother-of-pearl and sparkling gems, drew the eye.

"Well, Mr. American. What about this photo? What does it say to you?"

"I'm speechless."

"Indeed. There's a certain essence to a woman in her forties. Back then, I didn't truly grasp it, but now I'd give anything to embody that woman once more. They had abducted my second husband, Pavel, and myself. At the time of the photo, the ransom had been paid, and we were free. But the situation remained complex. Let's just say that negotiations were still very much in progress. Our people captured this photo to make a statement, or at least that's what I was told.

"Pavel started Genesis Security in retaliation for the kidnapping. When they captured us, we had what you westerners call 'kidnap and ransom insurance.' Our security detail was touted as the best money can buy and they were to keep us safe as we traveled the globe. We found out that arrangements like that work well until they fail catastrophically, like when kidnappers abducted us off the beach that night. In two days, they paid the criminals in US one-hundred-dollar bills. We paid the deductible like someone just hit our car and ran off, and the offender made a tidy amount for his efforts. Imagine insurance incentivizing the hit-and-run driver! Whoever paired insurance with ransom was a shortsighted fool. But alas, there are many idiots in the world, and they run things.

"Shortly after, we discovered that one of our own security team set us up to be taken. It read like a screenplay from a B movie. To dissuade suspicion, they bludgeoned the traitor on the head, and he suffered a convincing concussion—a small price for his future windfall. Of course, we would never be hurt—it was simply business. The insurance money was all they were after. However, revenge is an ugly enterprise, and setting an example is the only effective way of sending a message. The man and his entire family, along with the families of the two accomplices, were brutally murdered. Technically, I had no blood on my hands, but I regret I never found a way to save the children. I was told, 'Do not fret. Their lives reinforce our message.' So senseless! We do things differently now that I direct the company."

Val shifted her posture, bringing her hands together, her pose precisely matched the image. The same look in her eyes emerged, the only difference being twenty years. A chill ran down his spine, making him want to back away, but he stood his ground, glad she was not in possession of a sword.

"I tell you this only to explain why I know you are a multi-millionaire. You have secrets Julian. Secrets you even kept from your wife."

"What the hell's going on here? You can't possibly know what my net worth is. I'm not even sure!"

Val broke the pose and floated an arm into the air as she smiled and headed for the couch. "When Pavel died, I took over Genesis Security. We have ways of learning about people. Sometimes, we need to ensure kidnappings never happen, and sometimes, I need to know about who we wish to work with."

She leaned easily into the cushions, confident Julian would not leave. "I'm told you are a man of faith. Is that a coy reference to your deceased wife, Faith? I ask, because you have not attended church since the COVID pandemic."

"Look. I'm being more than patient, but I can see when somebody is trying to provoke me. What are you getting at?" Julian said.

"My interest is not to provoke you, I am impossibly curious. But are you truly one of the fortunate, who can find a way to believe in God?" She gestured kindly for him to sit down.

"Yes. I believe in God. So what?"

"As you know, I became an actress, but you would be unaware of how I was disgraced in Canne's in 1994. Pulp Fiction was the talk of the town and upstaged what was my most illustrious role." She shrugged. "It happens. But it was a foolhardy rendezvous with the President of the Jury that caused the tabloid scandal. From that, I could not recover. Devastated, I escaped back to Russia only to find myself crushed again. It was the same year Aleksandr Solzhenitsyn returned to Russia. No doubt convenient for the press, both of us were at the hotel Metropol at the same time. Unfortunately for me, however, they asked the great man if he admired the work of Anastasiya Valentina Volkov. The free press reported him as saying, 'I do not know that woman, but I am certain God does.'

"The axiom, *there's no such thing as bad publicity, is a* lie. When the USSR collapsed, Mosfilm went with it for a time. My contract ended and I had no safety-net," Val smiled, "other than my Soviet good looks. Reputation meant everything and mine was on the rocks, but I will not bore you with details."

It was the first time Julian had noticed the wrinkles in her face. Before, when she smiled, they boosted her vitality, coming from the corners of her eyes like radiant sunbursts, but now, those same accents that gave her life, fell into distress making her appear old.

"I only glimpsed Solzhenitsyn. They called him a saint—a holy man. I don't know. I tried reading his stuff, but it is too Russian for my tastes—melancholic and brooding. Still, I've envied true believers, and I sense he was one. A belief in forgiveness, hope and the spiritual essence of love sounds so idyllic. But I don't have the gene. After the events of 1989—'you would call it 'the fall of the iron curtain'—playing with the idea of religion was all the rage. I tried it on, but it did not fit. The Bolsheviks probably extracted the gene from my grandparents. Perhaps they will make a vaccine someday and I will be saved." She shuttered, and for an instant, her face took on a white pallor. "Oh Julian! I must apologize. Your wife died from a reaction to a vaccine, or so I am told. Not only am I destined to hell, I am thoughtless in life."

Julian struggled to trust her, and being reminded of her talents as an actress, did not help. Today's events seemed too orchestrated, and he felt manipulated, unsure of her motives. But it was the reminder of Faith that left him speechless. She returned his stare. It was apologetic yet analytical and made him uncomfortable. Eventually,

Val looked down, contrite. When she raised her head again, she was fully rejuvenated, her confidence restored, beaming with life.

"Enough about religion. I find it is the secrets people keep that make them truly interesting," Val said. "One advantage of running a world-class security company is having financial analysts. All I have to do is say, 'Find out everything about Julian James Comstock' and a file arrives in my inbox within the day. I'm surprised by a pattern in your actions. Given your background, I expected more caution with open ledger transactions. Yet, it seems you weren't hiding your long-term dollar-cost averaging in Bitcoin. With the meteoric growth and acceptance of cybercurrency, your net worth exceeds eighteen million dollars. Yes, Julian, you are rich. Faith didn't know because you kept it a secret from her, but I know, because the stakes are very high and I must know everything about the people I work with."

Chapter 11

SHE SMOOTHED THE SIDES of her dress with her hands as she stood up and walked to the fourth picture. "I'm having fun. Thank you for keeping me company and allowing me to be myself." Gently resting her hand on the frame of the last picture, Val's expression softened, revealing a vulnerability that seemed out of place.

"What do you see in this photo?"

It was the only black-and-white in the collection, and it evoked an eerie sensation within him. Her pose had her sitting, looking off into the distance, slumped forward and knees pulled up into her, with hands clasped around her right knee. The wedding band on her left ring finger was dead in the center of the photo, looming in a shadow. The emotion could be despair or pain—probably both. "I'd say you were hurting."

"That's all you've got?" Val questioned as she threw her hands into the air in exasperation. "Of course, I'm hurting. The vastness of humanity is hurting. This is not a model's pose—a friend took it with her phone. It was the day they killed Pavel Dmitri Popov. He was the only man I ever truly loved. The media called him an oligarch. Everyone thinks Russian oligarchs made their fortunes in oil, but my oligarch was a computer engineer. He leaked information in 2014 and became ridiculously wealthy. During your 2016 presidential election he sold tens of thousands of emails back to a certain lady who thought she had destroyed everything with bleaching software and a hammer. But my man couldn't leave well enough alone and offered proof that an inconvenient copy still existed. We were happy and well-off long before he waded into American political theater, but his willingness to chase down dirt on high-level diplomats paid absurd financial rewards. Unfortunately, his behavior placed him onto a long list of persons who knew too much. Pavel realized the position he had placed himself in, and it made him paranoid. In the best of times, he was a complicated man, but once he took to blackmailing corrupt dynasties, he fell to pieces.

"He had all the evidence to show that extorting the most powerful people in the world was a death sentence, but once he started, he could not stop. He began as a hacker and unlike you, he never changed his ways, even to his own destruction. So, he used the only mindset he knew and looked at his troubles through problem-solving, exploration and adaptability. It's why he divorced me and surrounded himself with more technology and information than his enemies.

"To protect me, he did the honorable thing and had a flamboyant affair with a Colombian pop star. Then he said ugly things about me before filing for divorce. It was an unconventional act of love. Pavel needed to separate me from his life to safeguard me from his fate. And it might have been a noble gesture if he had remained alive. Either way, the public nature of the humiliation regarding his infidelity did remove me from the chain of association. After all, I'm an actress, and acting the part of a woman scorned is child's play—the trick is to underplay the role.

"Of course, I tried to save our marriage and begged him to take me somewhere off-grid. We could escape and live like peasants—happy and together. But he would have none of it, convinced there was another option that suited his skill levels more. He built something that he was certain could out run his past mistakes. That's the reason I'm here. I must unload the albatross around my neck and I've found a proper home for it.

"In the divorce, I received this lovely yacht and more money than I could ever spend. When his plane crashed on takeoff from Samedan Airport in the Alps, I inherited two further gifts. One I love and one I curse. He named me trustee for Genesis Security and I found I have a knack for the job. His second gift is something far more insidious than anything I can control or make use of. It defies my understanding, and I could never bring myself to trust anyone to run it on my behalf. It is a quantum computer," she paused and appeared to study Julian's reaction.

"I found myself the unintended heir to his final, desperate chess move against those he had burned. But honestly, the stronger his security network and the smarter his computers, the more he came to realize he couldn't outwit a motivated assassin."

Julian said nothing and did not show that the news startled him. He knew he would have a million questions soon enough, but he also knew his silence would eventually encourage her to continue.

"At first, I considered destroying Pavel's ridiculous computer, but it was his dream even before he had the wealth necessary to create it. I'm glad he lived long enough to see the results of his work. But within weeks, he was dead and I was in charge of the damn thing. I decided to disconnect it. After settling the accounts of those involved, I had it placed aboard and sailed from Port Rashid. Now, I'm going to give it away, but that is none of your concern. I need you to focus on a task that's far from the complexities of quantum computing, grounded in a different kind of technology."

Chapter 12

"Your stories are intriguing and you have lived quite a fascinating life. But I'm still at a loss. I don't know what I'm doing here or why you have stolen me away from my life. What am I missing?" Julian asked.

"You're possibly lacking patience, yet your point stands. I admit, I've been a less than stellar host, immersed in the tales of my trials and heartaches. However, my goal has almost been realized. You know something about my past—pivotal moments that shape who I am. Now you need to know what makes me tick and why I appealed to Mitch to focus on you for so long leading up to today." A perfect smile signaled what could only be devious intent. "Did he really brandish his weapon at you?"

Julian sat on the edge of the couch, watching Val as she stopped pacing and looked at him, waiting for an answer. "You had to be there. You would think that kidnapping me, pulling a gun on me and throwing me overboard would all be hostile events, but there is something about Mitch that makes you want to give him the benefit of the doubt. Despite his actions, there does not seem to be any malice in his heart. I think he could be a friend if he wasn't working for you."

"Precisely. That is why I asked him to change his plans and sail into your marina. And look, you are here now. He did his job, but I have not done mine yet." She moved before a window and contemplated the coastline as they cruised slowly northward. "Mitch and I..." She changed her mind and continued on an alternate path. "The entire resistance movement accepts that civilization is in decline. History reveals the reason, if only we can look at it honestly. People desire many things, but we have the right to only one precious commodity—liberty. It may echo like a call from a bygone era, but bear with me and you will understand why my concerns are timeless."

She turned to face Julian, standing with impeccable posture, eyes intent on commanding all of his attention. It made him self conscious at first, but his mind cleared of distractions as he focused on what she had to say.

"In your beliefs, God created people, loving each one so much that He gave them free choice. We don't choose when we're born or when we die, but we do have control over our lives in between. I believe our fates aren't fixed, and our pleas are not heard by some divine entity, but a harsh, unforgiving natural law still rules us. Yet, in this unyielding truth, I see beauty in the innate freedom we're born with.

"But others battle against natural laws, insisting on their own. The harm we face doesn't come from our family or community, or even from individuals seeking to advance their plight. It comes from those who inflict their power over others. That's where society falls apart. When we are forced to exist under rules prescribed by tyrants—the result is barbaric.

"Julian, I have lived under evil regimes and have been ruled by others that committed unspeakable atrocities in the name of collective action for the common good. Those in positions of power always use the utopian end as the rationalization for draconian means. I will not say that we will achieve a utopia by dismantling the power structure of the world, but removing the systemic structures that the powerful elite have built is a start, allowing the opportunity for individuals to thrive."

She softened her stare and said nothing more, leaving Julian to contemplate her words. While none of these thoughts were new to him, the challenge they sparked remained unique. He faced a choice to dismiss all of what Val said or accept it in its entirety. A binary, without nuance and no middle ground.

"Look, I appreciate the whole *peace, love and freedom* sentiment all wrapped up in the *live-and-let-live* motto, but you say you want a different future, a more natural society without coercion." Worry lines creased his forehead. "Yet, here I am on your yacht, against my will, being pressed into what? A kind of benevolent bondage? From where I'm sitting, you are the powerful elite. Why do you think what you want is better than what we have?"

"You are absolutely correct. I am guilty of everything I accuse others of, with the most obvious—using the goal of freedom and personal liberty to justify any means. Hypocrisy has existed since man took to walking the earth—of that, I am sure. I am a provocateur, capable of incredible hypocrisy. My only defense is I want nothing in return for my work in destroying evil in this world. In fact, I presume imprisonment will come because of my actions—perhaps death. I'll be content with the outcome if I can take down a handful of the real villains. You see, my ambition goes beyond mere fatalism. I would never sacrifice another to save myself."

Her gaze trailed along an aqua-green stripe weaving across the carpet, and for a moment, her steps mirrored its path. Julian wondered if she was done with the conversation or simply deciding what to say next.

"Pavel blackmailed political tyrants who wreck the lives of millions. He became rich by uncovering their secrets and then even more rich by protecting them from public disgrace. I must remedy that, and I'll spend every penny I have and all of my life's energy to expose the heinous crimes these people perpetrate."

She walked over to Julian and kneeled before him on the lush carpet, taking his hands. "I am sorry for my tactics. There is nothing I can say in my defense other than we need you to help us succeed."

A single word crystallized in Julian's mind—*uncomfortable*. He yearned for any alternative to the current, disquieting moment—anything else. But despite his wishes, reality remained unchanged. She continued to kneel, with tears welling up in her eyes and streaming down her cheeks. She turned away, embarrassed. Releasing his hands, she gathered the hem of her dress and rose to her feet. She walked to an expansive window watching the passing shoreline. He was encouraged when her posture seemed to soften and was glad for the reflective silence that followed.

"That is marvelous. What is it called?"

From Julian's vantage point, he couldn't discern her focus, yet he felt a wave of relief seeing her apparent willingness, even eagerness, to shift topics, and he promptly seized the opportunity. He moved to stand at her side, trailing just enough to catch her gaze, yet maintaining a respectful distance.

"That is Deception Pass," Julian said.

"Deception Pass? You can't be serious!"

"That bridge is the connection between Whidbey Island and Fidalgo Island. And yes, seriously, the bridge spans Deception Pass."

"Real life is so rich. I am trying to convince you that my goals are worthy and necessary, and I'm struck by the majesty of a waterway passing between vast rocky cliffs, magnificent evergreens, and the intricate steel bridge that must be a hundred years old. And it's called Deception Pass!" Val spun around, and once again, she reached her hands out to grasp Julian's as if to bleed off unwanted momentum. The smile on her face radiated delight. "Julian! A screenwriter would discard this scene or at least change the name of the pass to be something more believable. Isn't the irony quite remarkable? I have only told you the truth! Yet I am doing it at Deception Pass."

As her breathing steadied, she commented with sudden interest, "Look at all those small boats! Do you think this yacht could navigate through this Pass of Deception? I must speak to the captain. I will be right back."

She ran like a ballerina, exiting stage right. *Uncomfortable*, resonated through his mind again, but this time, because she was gone.

Chapter 13

"THE AUTUMN LIGHT IS perfect! Come, Julian. You must join me on the fantail. The captain assures me he can accommodate my detour and still arrive in Roche Harbor for our appointment with Dr. Ou."

Val brushed past him, carrying a small assortment of colorful clothes on hangers. A woman in her forties, wearing the ship's uniform and a matching windbreaker, stood ready on the aft deck. She had a camera hanging on a strap around her neck, but her attention controlled a photo drone flying not ten feet away. Once positioned, she spoke into the headset mic, and the yacht began a slow swing towards the setting sun within its own length.

Val pulled Julian into her pose, "This will only take a second." As if on cue, the woman held her camera to her eye and snapped a dozen pictures of the two of them without a word of instruction and then returned her attention to the drone. "See, that was not so bad. Now, hold this. It will only take a few minutes. Just follow Cynthia's directions exactly, and we will be on our way before you know it." She handed Julian a flimsy disc covered with light-reflecting material, gold on one side and silver on the other.

Meanwhile, Val moved into the shadow created by the expansive overhang of the upper deck. No fuss about modesty—no undergarments either. She stood there, confidently picking out her next outfit. The stunning model didn't seem to notice or care, but

Julian felt embarrassed and diverted his eyes, blocking his view by lifting the reflector disc higher.

True to her word, the entire photoshoot, including wardrobe changes, concluded swiftly. Cynthia gathered the drone and vanished. What had rolled in like a sudden mist of vanity evaporated just as quickly. Val emerged adorned in white capri pants, a chambray shirt, and a long, open-front olive green cardigan.

"Thank you for indulging me. Now, even though the sun is setting, this day is not over—not even close. You have a lot to learn before you can make the decisions I need you to make. Come with me," Val said.

He had put away the idea of diving overboard and swimming to safety when the image had popped into his head earlier, but he did stare longingly towards the rocky shore before following his confounding host into the warm expanse of the yacht's salon.

"I'd like you to meet Justin," Val began. "Pavel found him living in an unsavory part of Damascus when he was just a boy. A computer genius, an extraordinary protege and now, he is family. I have asked him to attend to your needs and answer any questions you have."

Val continued, "I must prepare for the hand-off. Finally, I'll be rid of Pavel's ridiculous quantum computer. Even Justin here agrees with my decision. How did you phrase it?"

Val turned her gaze to Justin, encouraging him to respond like a teacher coaxing a shy student. Justin's face shifted into a smirk as he recited, "*Rain nourishes crops, but storms destroy the farm.* It seemed fitting at the time, but now I wish I had kept my mouth shut."

"Oh, darling, don't sell yourself short," Val assured him.

Julian wasn't surprised by Val's appraisal as it progressed the notion of a teacher-student relationship. Justin's embarrassment, however, appeared more childlike. His high-pitched voice, slight build, and stature confirmed his youthfulness. He stood a couple of inches shorter than Val, and while his straight black hair appeared clean, it looked like it had been cut drastically about a year ago and then left without a trim. His skin reflected his Mediterranean origin. Justin's strong accent confirmed his Syrian connections, but his English was perfect.

Justin didn't dress like a typical crew member. He was wearing red Converse sneakers and blue jeans ripped at the knees, along with a black T-shirt featuring the iconic AC/DC logo. This kind of outfit would fit in with his age group anywhere in the world, but on an elegant megayacht, it just felt out of place. He looked to be about eighteen, but exuded an air of competence that reminded Julian of the most-skilled students at the University of Washington.

Their assessment was fleeting. Eyes briefly meeting in a silent acknowledgment of their mutual wish to be elsewhere. Julian offered a friendly smile, which Justin met with an indifferent nod before redirecting his attention to Val.

She conversed with Justin in what Julian surmised to be Arabic, their words flowing effortlessly. Justin turned towards Julian, bowed his head slightly, then walked away with hurried steps.

Earlier, Val's movements had been accentuated by the silkiness of her dress. Now, her casual outfit radiated a sense of laid-back ruggedness. Julian couldn't dismiss the possibility that she could perform any role she wanted.

She spoke with a matter-of-fact tone, obviously not wanting to be underestimated. "I told him to get you a secure device for accessing the information you need to make an informed decision. Forgive me, but I can't allow you outside communications until we agree on your future. Still, you'll receive the details about our rebellion. I'm confident that once you see and hear the truth, you'll eagerly join our efforts.

"The captain says we'll be in port soon, and I must prepare for my meeting. Justin will return shortly, so if you require anything, just ask. Our surveillance is like your god—omnipresent."

He watched as she began to leave the room. "I don't believe you have a quantum computer," Julian said to her back.

She spun and returned the look of disbelief. "Very well, I will show you. Before I deliver it to its new owner. It is quite the novelty." This time, her steps resonated with determination, each one almost a march as she moved away.

Julian wondered if Justin had been waiting for Val to leave before he returned with the *secure device*. This time, along with a sincere smile, the boy was wearing a royal blue baseball cap with a crisp, straight brim and ATARI printed in bold white letters across the front. He handed Julian an iPad and a bowl filled with what looked like trail mix.

"The chef prepares this for me. She says it is computer food." He glanced at the iPad apologetically. "It's the only thing with a CPU that security would let me bring you. I loaded it with what Val wants you to see." He winced, turned and walked away.

The device, loaded with a single application, drew Julian's focus to a rotating pyramid graphic at the center of the screen. Exploring what they wanted him to find might come later. His first mission was to hack the infernal device. Within minutes, Julian was desperate for a keyboard and mouse, but eventually, he settled into a flow with the touch interface. Breaking out of kiosk mode was simple, but accessing the ship's internet proved impossible, until he thought of Cynthia's photo drone. He wondered if it might be charging somewhere close by. If he managed to hack into its Wi-Fi connection, it would provide the necessary intermediary device to relay the internet to his iPad.

Chapter 14

"Do you think this is too much?" Val asked as she spun around for Julian to take in her outfit.

"What is it you're going for?"

"Faith was a lucky woman. A man with good looks and a brain." She lowered her hands and said, "I'm meeting the world-famous inventor of the Madras Motor, Olin Ou, and his family, so I'm wanting to be a bit more conservative and family-friendly than I actually am. But then, there is a bit of intrigue to the evening's encounter as I am smuggling a priceless gem into a country which does not appreciate the voluntary exchange of such things. Do I look the part?"

"Well, then—you are perfect," Julian said and turned his attention back to the iPad.

"I retract that. Your wife, may she rest in peace, had to endure what all women deal with. A man who says the right thing for the wrong reasons."

This interchange was precisely the banter he would have had with Faith, and much like now, he was always on the losing end of the battle. But instead of making him more cautious, he felt a warmth overtake him. "Okay, you're right. When I said you're perfect, I meant it. You are stunning, and your outfit just complements that. From what I can tell, you are wearing the same thing you were wearing after your photoshoot, only you exchanged the green sweater for this deep red one that has a hood. It is a good look and fits in well with the boating community here in the Pacific Northwest. You will please the eyes but not attract unwanted attention."

Val raised her right hand to her chest and exhaled as if she had been holding her breath during his entire pronouncement. The relief on her face appeared genuine—she blushed and retrieved an Amish-woven pie basket from a nearby countertop. He knew nothing about baskets but recognized the style because there was one very much like it on *Horizon's Edge* that currently held every wool sock he owned.

"I told you I would show you my quantum computer." She lifted the wooden lid to reveal a stainless steel box. "Here it is," she said.

Julian noted the perturbed tone of her voice, but he couldn't let his challenge fade. "I'm sorry, but a quantum computer, even the most cutting-edge examples, require entire rooms to contain them."

"Oh, thank you for the lesson in computer mechanics, Professor Comstock." She rolled her eyes. "Dr. Ou is one of the most brilliant men on the planet. He has already designed a cooling system that is superior to anything Pavel could have imagined, and let's just say, the energy requirements—well, he is an electrical engineer who designed the most efficient motor in the history of mankind. This, Julian, is the extraordinary heart of Pavel's computer—the quantum processor. And that, darling, is how we roll." She returned the lid to the basket top, drew up the handles and walked past Julian with her chin held high.

"Okay, maybe," Julian said. "Are you going to be pulling that hood up on your way over there? With that basket, you've got the whole Little Red Riding Hood vibe."

Val stopped in her tracks, turned her head enough for Julian to see the gleam in her eye. "More like Granny."

Julian approached her, iPad in hand. He raised the screen so she could see the picture. "Who is this?" The image showed a distorted, low resolution image of a woman wearing a blue baseball cap, her expression serious and somewhat imposing.

Val set her basket down on the floor and grabbed the device with both hands. "How did you get this picture?"

"Remember. I'm a hacker. You knew that, and I'm guessing that's why I'm here."

"But our security is... and it's only been minutes..." She fell into silence.

"I captured this image from my daughter's doorbell camera. She's the one who abducted Jonathan, Emily's boyfriend. Who is she?"

Val pushed the device back into Julian's hands. "There is no reason for me to tell you."

"What about all that talk about transparency and getting to know each other—friends and all?" Julian said with a note of sarcasm.

"You're right. I will have Justin provide anything you need. I must remind you, however, there are many lives at stake here, including children—especially children. I'm trusting you, in order that you can trust me." Her eyes darted towards the iPad. "Her name is Julie Marsh. She is one of ours—Genesis Security. Before she joined us, she rose to the rank of Command Sergeant Major in the US Army—she is not a rookie—but clearly unaccustomed to the vulnerability doorbell security cameras pose. We will bring her up to our expectations, and a mistake like this will not happen again. Thank you for bringing this lapse to my attention." She grabbed her basket and walked away without another word, her deck shoes making no sound.

Chapter 15

"The next room is *The Ballast*," Justin said.

Julian thought it strange, as they were nowhere near the keel of the boat, but said nothing.

"Personally, I've never been interested in the reason for the name. My coworkers laugh and say it is where the heavy work occurs. Whatever."

Julian had overheard Val speaking to Justin as she was leaving the boat. He couldn't make out their words, but the tone was clear enough—Val was upset, her angst directed at Justin.

With no enthusiasm, Justin led him down a flight of stairs, showed him the dining room and gave him a peek into the large galley. They walked through a compact workout gym that looked down into a full-sized racquetball court. With each step through the megayacht, Justin's pace suggested he wanted to be anywhere else. Convinced that the young man's appointment as his personal tour guide was a burden, Julian asked, "Is everything alright?"

"I'm being punished because of you. It's Cedric's job to show guests around." Justin turned and looked into Julian's eyes. "Why did you hack that iPad I gave you? You made me look bad."

"It wasn't personal. I needed more information than Val would give me."

A sardonic grin stretched across Justin's face. "Have you ever been tased?"

"*Tased*?"

"You know, like this." Justin stiffened, quivering slightly, his eyes rolling back comically to mimic an electrical charge moving through his body.

"No, I've never been tased," Julian admitted.

"Well, it hurts. If security on this ship ever stops you with a Taser, I guarantee, there is someone else standing-by, ready to shoot you with lead. We have a walk-in freezer and it has plenty of room for your body."

Everything about the threat took Julian by surprise. He had misunderstood Justin, mistaking him for a teenager due to his short stature and sparse facial hair. However, he now recognized that Justin was older than he seemed. Adding to the confusion, the words Justin spoke sounded menacing, yet his tone and high-pitched voice were anything but intimidating.

"If you make Val mad, you make everybody angry," Justin continued.

"Was she mad?"

"Are you clueless?" Justin rolled his eyes. "It took a month before she cleared me to work in The Ballast. Believe me, she's only giving you access because you infuriate her, and she doesn't know what else to do with you." He stopped before activating the key-pad for the entry. "Good luck inside there. If they don't like you, they'll eat you alive." Justin opened the heavy door, walked into the room and gestured for Julian to follow.

"Here, this is your workstation." Justin pointed to the empty chair and simple computer setup on a sit-stand desk. He directed his attention across the aisle. "That's Marco, he's an American, and Demetri the Russian is back there. You've already met. When he's not pulling people out of the water, he is the head of cybersecurity."

Before Justin turned to leave, his face softened and before he could shut the door behind him, Julian realized Justin could not hold a grudge.

The room was not large but had plenty of space. Marco didn't budge and occupied the workstation directly opposite Julian's. They would be back-to-back after he took his seat, but for now, he could see each of Marco's screens, and with only a glance, knew this guy was into some serious coding. Demetri's station, at the far end of the room, faced them. Half a dozen monitors blocked his view, so he half-stood up and waved, but with no smile.

Marco finally looked up from his work, his screens went dark, and he stared at Julian as if his eyes could not resolve the image. Eventually, Julian broke the awkward gaze and sat in his chair.

"It looks like we'll be eating here tonight," Marco declared, his Brooklyn accent adding a gruff undertone. "The chef is off to get supplies, so the ship's galley is closed. Thanks to you, we're getting takeout. Here, use this." He handed Julian a tablet. "Pick anything you want, but do it now."

The screen showed the menu for the *Madrona Bar and Grill*. He selected the box for *Tilted Kettle Clam Chowder* and then hesitated as he saw an item that he could not believe—*Local Rockfish and Chips*. "How do they get permission to serve local, wild caught fish? That requires a special UN permit. I hear it's like getting a writ from the king to hunt in his forest—near impossible."

"Look at the price on the menu," Marco said. "Did you see the yachts around this marina? Hell, did you notice the size of *Elysium Prime*? Permission and cost is of no consequence to the rich, they get what they want. Choose anything that catches your eye. Our wealthy benefactor is footing the bill. Just hurry it up, I'm hungry."

Julian hit the submit button, and said, "Done."

"What, do you want a medal?" Marco said. "I have some ideas about how you leaped over our firewall so fast, but just so you know, you ruined everything with your stunt." Marco's eyes darted around as he spoke to Julian. He wasn't much older than Justin, maybe twenty-five, and his long hair trailed down his neck, competing with tattoos emerging upward from the collar of a black t-shirt.

But it was his New York accent that appeared to Julian as his most distinguishing feature.

"We were going to get an evening onshore—an open tab at the bar. Justin has never stepped foot in America before, and he turned twenty-one two days ago. It was time for us to celebrate, but now, we need to study your ways and learn from the master." Marco performed a mocking bow in Julian's general direction. "I hope you like Linux. Use this ever-changing password." He tossed Julian an inch-long stainless tube with a red-blinking digital readout that appeared to shine through the metal. "It only operates in this room."

When the characters changed into a steady green, he logged in, revealing only one icon on the screen. The same one he had seen on the iPad. His gut told him to ignore what they wanted him to see and start digging into the stuff they were hiding. While Justin's comment about getting tased didn't scare him, he proceeded with more caution and decided to give Val a chance. He assumed the icon led to some sort of recruitment presentation and wondered if he didn't owe her at least that? The idea was ludicrous—he owed her nothing. With a sigh of resignation, he pulled on the high-end, noise-canceling headphones and clicked the slowly rotating pyramid in the middle of his screen.

An amorphic synthesized voice said, "Good evening, Mr. Comstock. My intention is to answer your initial questions. There are several directions in which we could begin: Economic, including macroeconomics; health, including public health; and, where most people wish to begin, political discourse. Fear not. You have as much time with me as you desire, and we can carry on with a simple survey of the data or dive deep into the details. Val has instructed me to follow your lead and answer any preliminary questions you might have. Please let me know where you would like to begin."

"From the beginning," he said, wondering if he should have asked for the abbreviated version.

The blasé default Linux screen transformed into a high-definition theater without titles or introductions. A sprawling courtyard fringed with buildings of Gothic architecture held hundreds of people. Some passed purposefully, as if late for class, while others mingled, studied on benches or sat in the shade of stately trees. It was a scene that could represent many university campuses throughout the world, but the casual attire, lack of physical distancing, and absence of any masking, even in large groups, showed a time before fear-driven rhetoric and lockdowns prevailed. Julian couldn't help himself. The smiles on the faces of the co-eds proved contagious. It was a wonderful scene reminding him of his own years in college. He felt sad for today's students. Years of robbing joy out of the hearts of young people had taken its toll. No campus looked this idyllic today. Julian glanced to his left and behind him as he remembered he was not alone in the room. The others stayed absorbed in their work. He returned to the view just as a beam of light concentrated over the scene.

"Welcome, Julian. My name is Rivenna. I am an educational AI." The light came to life, casting shimmering lights upon the surrounding building. Her voice stood in stark contrast to the synthesized voice at the opening of the presentation. This voice sounded fully human. It resonated through the open courtyard, but nobody paid attention to it.

"I have studied your curriculum vitae. Your degree is in computer science, but you have had a fine classical liberal education, and are well-traveled throughout Europe and the Americas. Based on your audio book library, your subscriptions and book order history, your economic knowledge is above average, and your grasp of history is excellent. However, you are lacking in political science and current affairs. I have collected information which should fill in some gaps and get you up to speed without boring you with details. After this brief presentation, I trust you will have a better understanding of liberty and personal freedoms. In addition, I have outlined some of the principal threats to these hard-won values. It is critical to acknowledge both the journey of humanity's quest for liberty and the shadows that seek to extinguish its light."

As Rivenna narrated, Julian observed the screen, where the courtyard and its inhabitants seamlessly transformed into a vivid montage. This visual journey unfolded at the pace of her storytelling.

In the rich tapestry of ancient times, the profound wisdom of Solomon laid foundational stones in the East, while in the West, spurred by the visionary ideals of Pericles, ancient Greece thrived and sowed the seeds of democracy. The scene transitioned to the Roman Republic, where legal innovations shaped enduring systems of justice. Images of Enlightenment philosophers debating revolutionary ideas filled the screen, symbolizing an era of intellectual awakening and the rejection of traditional authorities. The American Revolution, ignited by a fervent desire for self-determination and freedom, gave birth to foundational documents like the Declaration of Independence and the U.S. Constitution, illuminating the path toward democracy and inspiring future generations in their quest for liberty. The montage shifted to the fight against slavery worldwide, convincing the world that freedom and equality are the natural state for all people, and anything else, should never be tolerated.

The screen portrayed people rising against distant colonial rulers, passionately seeking independence and breaking free from oppressive yokes. It showed movements advocating for women's rights, highlighted Mahatma Gandhi's nonviolent resistance, depicted Martin Luther King Jr.'s fight for civil rights, and showcased Lech Wałęsa's pivotal role in Poland's Solidarity Movement

Throughout this audiovisual journey, the relentless pursuit of freedom and justice highlighted the indomitable spirit of individuals and nations. The profound human longing for liberty and the rejection of oppressive rule resonated deeply with Julian.

Rivenna did not miss a beat and continued narrating along with the video storyboard. "In the ever-evolving tapestry of history, we witness more recent movements toward freedom, where people from all walks of life have risen to confront oppressive regimes and champion liberty. The Arab Spring, with its passionate calls for democracy and the global push for human rights, exemplify the relentless human spirit in its pursuit of freedom and equality. These modern chapters, coupled with the timeless stories of those who fought for liberty, continue to inspire individuals to work towards a brighter future for all."

As these scenes of triumph receded, a darker tapestry unfurled. "It would be irresponsible to ignore the ever-present threats to liberty. Throughout human history, a revolutionary spirit and awareness of the hazards which appear innocuous, or even progressive, is required to combat the insidious evil."

Amidst the changing scene, words floated in from the lower right to center screen: "Government Overreach." The title spun out of view, replaced with the bleak walls of dystopian cities, where chains bound their citizens. Skyscrapers towered like watchful overlords.

"When the government loses sight of the sacred value of the individual, influential political elites and hardliners manipulate policies while citizens' freedoms slowly erode beneath the weight of intrusive regulations until the people no longer have a voice. They become subjects, barely tolerated, often abused and always powerless."

"Authoritarianism" drifted across the screen. Grim images showcased societies where voices were silenced, books burned and history rewritten. "They snuff out cherished liberties under authoritarian shadows," Rivenna warned.

The next title dropping in from the center top was "Tech Surveillance." Scenes shifted to depict eyes within every device and on cameras on every street corner. Technology has been a double-edged sword. In the wrong hands, it becomes an apparatus to spy on citizens and undermine autonomy."

"Social Conformity" faded into the screen and quickly faded out again, leaving a chilling visual of individuals morphing into identical entities. "Societal pressures fanned by powerful elites and corporate-funded media outlets have forced unique identities into a ubiquitous mold, causing the rich diversity of expression and thought to become stifled."

The word "Justice" rolled in from center left as "Inaccessibility" met it from center right. As the phrase "Justice Inaccessibility" disappeared, a courtroom setting morphed into the symbolic scales of justice with a ghoulish hand manipulating the imbalance. "The average person's plea for fairness is lost in a maze of corruption and influence.

"In the 20th century, the world witnessed significant ideological struggles, including the rise and fall of communism and the dramatic dissolution of the Soviet Union, both of which had a profound impact on the global landscape and the ongoing debate surrounding liberty and personal freedoms."

The title "Crisis Impact" tumbled into view. Images of chaos flooded the screen—natural disasters, wars, and pandemics played out with a shadowy overlay of a firm hand tightening its grip. "Emergencies are the fertile ground where liberties are curtailed and never returned," Rivenna intoned.

"Global Challenges" came next. A world map showing hot spots of conflict and pulsating colors representing opposing tensions, followed by a puppeteer's strings manipulating the scene. "Global issues, under the guise of collective security, are used to threaten individual freedoms and justify oppression."

A sun rising out of a dark purple screen, cast a hopeful mood following the intensity of the presentation. "Julian, thank you for paying such close attention to my presentation. If we are to value liberty and respect personal freedoms, then we must realize the tactics of those who have evil intent. As threats play out, our resolve erodes, and our ability to precipitate change diminishes. A rallying spirit is essential to maintain hard-won progress," Rivenna proclaimed. "Each freedom-loving individual must make a choice—how far am I willing to go?"

The screen filled with a silver and gold fractal as Rivenna continued. "We hope that you have found liberty to be the highest of human endeavors. We also trust you understand the threats from those who wish to control others. And while the revolutionary spirit is alive—it is not well. What appeared to be an indomitable human force has given way to social helplessness and a desire to be coddled from cradle to grave. A commitment to entitlement has replaced rugged individualism and self-mastery, while a lack of expectations has co-opted timeless values. Julian, the powerful have stolen so much. They have bought and connived their way into control, but we can still make a difference. We need you to be ready to protect the flame of freedom."

The screen faded out with the last image of many hands of varying colors and sizes holding a single torch burning an eternal flame.

Julian didn't exactly know why, but he found himself choked up—a little too emotional. He looked behind him and over toward the end of the room to find his new coworkers still busy with their own tasks. Nobody was paying any attention to him. Clearly, the AI had honed in on ideals that resonated with him. He knew propaganda the moment he saw it, and he understood marketing enough to sense he was being worked into a particular state of mind, but he couldn't dismiss the content presented. It was intended to manipulate his decision about joining Val's band of quasi-revolutionaries, but it didn't have any effect on his decision. He already knew all these things. The experience of living in an eroding city and working on a faltering campus, gave him the pulse of the society—weak—despite its arrogance. Rivenna had just validated convictions he already possessed.

Chapter 16

"WHAT KIND OF BEER do you drink?"

"What?" Julian said, startled by the voice coming through his headphones. He took them off and spun his chair around to see Marco looking at him.

"The ship's galley is closed," Marco said. "But you can still get a beer. What do you want?"

"Actually, I'll take some water. Is there coffee?"

Marco grinned and gestured toward Julian's right. Just a few steps away, embedded in the wall, stood a sleek glass-fronted refrigerator. Inside, an array of soft drinks, water, and even a modest assortment of sandwiches, wraps, fruit, and cheese plates were clearly visible. What surprised him most was not the visibility of its contents, but that he hadn't noticed it until now.

"Coffee." Marco pointed to another obvious kiosk on the other side of the aisle which included drip coffee, tea, a condiment bar and even a small espresso machine. "Dinner's arriving in five minutes."

Julian took a chilled carafe from the refrigerator, broke the seal and filled a glass with water. He picked a mug from a small collection and then saw the writing on the side and said, "Demitri, this must be yours. Right?"

The Russian's head peeked over the monitors. This time he smiled. "Go ahead. It's for you. From me. A gift." He chuckled as he noticed Julian's confusion over the Cyrillic script.

"It says, roughly translated, *I love sarcasm. It's like punching people in the face, but with words,*" Demitri laughed, as he stood up from his station and approached Julian.

No one could miss that Demitri was broad-shouldered, but this was the first time Julian had stood next to him. He was easily six-foot-five and solid muscle, but the imposing sight didn't stop there. Strapped to the left side of his belt was a pistol and on the right was a Taser. Julian stepped back instinctively.

Demitri patted Julian gently on the shoulder as he picked another mug. He put a tea-bag into it and filled it with steaming water from a tap, then held it up for him to see. "Do you know what this one says?" Not waiting for an answer, he read, "*Cybersecurity: The Few. The Proud. The Paranoid.*" He was still laughing as he disappeared behind his bank of monitors.

There was a muffled knock on the door. Julian looked to see Justin standing there, smiling, with two large bags of food. Marco got up and opened it. "I'm eating in the breakroom. That means you have to join me. From now on, where you go, I go, and where I go, you go." Marco held the door open for Julian to follow.

"How are your studies?"

"What studies?" Julian said.

As they sat down in the nondescript breakroom, Marco said, "I haven't been read into all this, but when I'm told to allow the new guy access to everything, and then Demitri is told to shoot him if he tries anything, something's big—you're important, but not trusted. I just want to know why.

"You got your own AI-driven introduction to liberty, and it didn't last all that long, so you're fairly well-educated in history and civics. I'd guess you lean libertarian or at least classical liberal. But it wasn't as short as mine—I'm an anarchist. Not much needs to be said there." He took a bite of his burger and finished his thought while chewing. "So, what do they want you to do?" He swallowed. "Save the world?"

Justin joined them at the table. If he maintained any lingering resentment towards Julian, it dissolved once he began to eat. However, this improvement in his demeanor didn't prevent him from voicing his opinion even before Julian had the chance to contemplate a response to Marco's question.

"The only person allowed to save the world is Val. We all are her minions. It works because I want to get rich, Marco wants to burn the world down, and Demitri is still bent on revenge for Pavel's assassination and..."

"Shut up, Justin. You don't know what you're talking about," Marco said.

"I'm not stupid."

"No, you're brilliant. But you're too single-minded to figure out when you have it good. Val adores you like a son... or a grandson. We're all okay with that, so why aren't you? The nicer she is to you, the more of a prick you become."

Julian felt the tension as the two obviously resumed an unfinished conflict. He took a bite of fish, chewing slowly, trying to stay quiet.

Marco changed the subject and asked Justin, "Do you know why Julian is here? He claims his hacker days are behind him, but Val must want him for something. The old guy sure had no problem jail-breaking your iPad."

"I'm right here," Julian said, holding up a french fry covered in ketchup.

"Yeah, we can see that, but you've got nothing. You've only made us look bad, and as far as I can tell, you haven't helped advance our cause."

"Probably something to do with the shipment we picked up in Port Angeles at the time we cleared customs," Justin said.

"Why would he have anything to do with a bunch of computers that were made before we were born?" As the words came out of Marco's mouth, his jaw dropped and his eyes locked on Julian.

"You've got to be kidding me," Julian said. "What kind of computers?"

"Commodore 64s," Justin answered.

In disbelief, Julian lowered his head into the palm of his left hand. He held it there for a moment. When he looked up, both men were staring, waiting for him to speak. "When I was a kid, that's one of the types of computers I used to... hack stuff."

Marco and Justin smiled at each other.

"Did they come with dial-up modems?" Julian asked.

"What's a dial-up modem?"

Marco reached across the table and pretended to smack Justin's head. "If you'd actually learned your computer science in a school, you'd know. Think of it like an ancient version of Wi-Fi, using phone lines."

Justin smiled with a confused look. "Phone lines?"

The joke lightened the mood, but Julian couldn't let the question go. Again, he asked, "Are there modems?"

"There were a couple of other boxes that just said, *Hayes Microcomputer Products*. Is that what you're asking about?"

"Yep. That's a dial-up modem." Julian sighed. "This is unreal."

"I know I've never been to university, but why do you guys look like you've seen a ghost?"

"I'm as lost as you," Marco admitted. "Julian, it's time you talked."

"There's not much to say. I was in the 414s, an early band of hackers named after our area code. Dial-up was our gateway. We explored everything accessible through it. It was easy back then."

"Did you get caught?"

"We did, but not for a long time. They didn't do much to us. The closest thing they could charge us with was making prank phone calls, but nobody was convicted with anything significant. At least not then. They did take our equipment and banned us from the computer labs at our high school. They definitely tried to scare us. I guess it worked, I never really hacked anything again."

Both men looked skeptical.

Julian laughed. "Well, I steered clear of illegal hacks. Like, I stopped looking for points-of-entry weaknesses in government systems." A cautious grin formed on Julian's face as if he were telling a tall tale in the light of a campfire. "In the US anyway."

Justin stared at Julian in disbelief, and Marco mused, "You lived before they had laws against hacking. You are so freaking old!"

Feeling his years more than ever, Julian savored the last bite of the exceptional fish and chips, grasped his new mug and resolved, "Looks like we're in for a long night. Time to get down to business."

Chapter 17

"Well, look what we have here. It looks like Christmas day—in 1984—at least in America..." Val trailed off with a thoughtful look. "I see you boys have figured out what we're up to. Demitri, what have you told them?"

All attention shifted to the imposing figure seated cross-legged on the floor. "Don't look at me, I'm just here to breathe life back into these old dinosaurs." He mumbled something in Russian.

Val said a few words back to Demitri and then addressed the rest of the room in English with a laugh, "Allow me to paraphrase." Lowering her voice in an impersonation of Demitri she said, "I am spy. Don't expect blabbermouth."

"Did everyone get something to eat?" she asked. "While I've been off the *Elysium Prime*, the most enjoyable family has wined, dined and entertained me. Olin Ou and his delightful wife, Maria, have four children. The youngest are twin girls. Sidney is precocious, eager and curious. Nadia is the reticent one—she doesn't miss a thing. If she was twenty instead of ten, I'd recruit her for Genesis. Irina is fourteen going on twenty-one and has her father's passion for sailing."

Val reached into her basket and pulled out a tall package and placed it on the table. "This was dessert. The oldest, Marshall, is a wizard in the kitchen. Cowboy cookies! Americans are so creative." She untied a string and opened the parchment wrapping revealing a stack of oversized cookies with colorful M&M's and chunks of chocolate, with coconut and oats adding texture. "Marshall presented the cookies and said, 'dig in.' So creative. Why don't you—*dig in*? After all, we are in the states now." She gestured as if tipping an imaginary cowboy hat. "I'll be hittin' the trail for a spell, but I'll circle back in a few minutes. Demitri, be ready. We're gonna need to saddle up."

Julian was the last to reach for a cookie because his gaze lingered on Val as she walked out of the room. He observed a playful swagger in her step and he appeared to be the only one who noticed her subtle, almost bow-legged gait.

Demitri got up from the floor and went to his station. Standing straight and formal, he produced a conductor's baton and tapped the top of his monitor counsel three times. Classical music filled the room. Julian could not identify the score, but it was a lively and intricate composition. The wall behind him retracted, revealing another room with similar dimensions as The Ballast, but instead of desks and workstations, half a dozen leather chairs faced a small stage. The bright colors of a music visualization that reminded Julian of a screen saver from the nineteen-nineties filled the expansive presentation wall from floor to ceiling. Facing the audience was a single chair with oversized armrests similar to Captain Kirk's chair from Star Trek. The music quieted, and the display became an innocuous wall.

Demitri replaced the baton on his desk, turned and walked between the chairs, carrying a tablet device in one hand and a water glass in the other. He assumed the position of a presenter off to the side of the room and extended his arm holding the glass of water off to the side. A simple robotic arm extended out of the wall and provided a shelf. Demitri let go without looking, confident the water glass would not fall to the floor.

"What the heck?!" Marco questioned. "I've been on board for what? Half a year, and never knew this room existed."

"Pavel hired me for computer security, but when he found me, I was a spy," Demitri smirked. "I'm very good at keeping secrets."

Marco shot him an incredulous look. "I thought you were one of us."

"I came for the money, but stayed for the revolution." Demitri laughed as he took a moment to approach Marco. "We are brothers in this. You will see." It looked like Demitri was going to hug Marco but settled on placing a gentle hand on his shoulder.

Marco shrugged it off while saying, "Whatever. We're good. Let's get on with this. I'm just tired of being the last one to know what's going on."

Chapter 18

It had been difficult to pull himself away from the vintage computers and hardware. The revealed presentation room with Demitri commanding the space drew him in. Julian couldn't help recalling a familiar sensation from his youth when his mother insisted he leave his computer to join the family for dinner.

The glow of the cathode-ray-tube monitor emitted lines of nostalgic white characters against a bright blue background. For the first time in four decades, he read the start screen.

```
    **** COMMODORE 64 BASIC V2 ****
 64K RAM SYSTEM 38911 BASIC BYTES FREE
READY.
■
```

In the early eighties it was something he ignored, even disliked, but now the screen rekindled fond memories of countless hours spent exploring the world from his childhood bedroom. But now, a sealed box rested on the floor under his workspace, harboring an Epson dot matrix printer, the same model he had mowed lawns for during his senior year in high school. Its printouts comprised of interconnected ink dots, striving to pass as legible letters and numbers, evoking recollections of quirky, never-ending perforated paper scrolls. This entire setup mirrored precisely what the FBI had confiscated from him at seventeen. He purged the antiquated technology from his mind and forced himself to settle into an open chair.

Val walked in and took her place in the captain's chair as if it were a throne. But there was no pretension of formality, though when her eyes met Julian's, she did not smile. He noticed another wardrobe change. If she had asked him to comment, he wouldn't have to think what to say. Her goal was comfort. Ballet flats, loose-fitting jeans, a cream v-neck t-shirt, and an unbuttoned flannel shirt with sleeves folded partway. She even had her hair out of the way tucked into a messy ponytail.

She rotated her chair facing the wall sized screen. "Let's start with Dr. Talgat Kozhaev. Demitri, make the screen smaller. I don't want to see the monster's nose hairs."

A series of images appeared of a dark-haired man with a mustache. He was probably in his mid-forties, but had avoided any middle-age softening. A video showed him playing tennis as Demitri, standing off to one side, began an informal narration. "Dr. Talgat Kozhaev earned his medical credentials from Al-Farabi Kazakh National University in Almaty, Kazakhstan. He descends from a lineage of influential leaders. His father served as the Akim of Eastern Kazakhstan and his grandfather held the post of Chairman of the Executive Committee prior to Kazakhstan's independence from the USSR. For generations, the Kozhaevs have been pivotal in the region's administration, cementing themselves as not only the most authoritative family in the area, but also one of its wealthiest. While Talgat's brother, Baurzhan, has followed the family's political trajectory, Dr. Talgat Kozhaev has carved out his own influential sphere, amassing considerable wealth and power in his own right."

The screen shifted from family images to a red mosaic of animated blood cells that seemed to spill into the foreground. Demitri continued his discourse about the doctor. Julian could tell they were traveling within the arterial environment of the human body, but had no further understanding of what he was looking at other than cells reducing to particles and particles reducing to molecules.

"Initially recognized as a brilliant hematologist, Kozhaev, early in his career, stayed dedicated to rigorous research resulting in over a dozen peer-reviewed publications centered on conventional transfusion medicine. But then, his focus shifted radically towards life extension, tech evolution and trans-humanism. His methodologies, which sacrificed countless animals for what he termed *the beneficiary*, were met with skepticism due to ethical concerns. Over time, he ceased publishing his research and embarked on a journey to market his unique blend of art, science and philosophy to those with the deepest pockets."

A succession of photographs, brief video snippets and select news clips lit up the screen. As Demitri dropped the names of globally renowned figures, Julian realized he recognized many of these world leaders, celebrated actors, and industry titans. A vibrant circle encompassed their images as he announced each one. Yet, whenever Dr. Talgat Kozhaev's image appeared, it was surrounded by a conspicuous, deep-red circle. Demitri continued, "His global networking began as the presenter at a closed parallel session for the World Economic Forum in Davos, Switzerland. After that, observers began connecting the dots, noting Kozhaev's remarkable proximity to global leaders from various regimes. It is intriguing to note he gained US citizenship, and his frequent visits to Washington, D.C. coincided with a notably aged administration. At the time, the President was seventy-nine, Speaker of the House aged eighty-two, and a Senate Majority Leader, seventy-one."

"Demitri, we don't need your speculation. Stick to the facts and go on, but no more inferences to old people—I'm sensitive about age." Val swiveled her chair in Julian's direction, smiled and gave him a wink.

"Our involvement began after Stan Oberland, a Genesis Security bodyguard, informed us of our clients' illicit activity regarding child trafficking. Val, would you like to elaborate?" Demitri asked.

"I'm your gal." She turned to face her small audience. "Genesis Security has a broad range of services, one of them is as bodyguards to VIPs. Unfortunately, the world rewards some of the worst creatures and makes them *Very Important People*. Or, perhaps they become that way once they are among the elite. I believe it is the former, but either way, we often protect awful people. Of course, our security company has standards." She screwed up her face, continuing, "Admittedly, they are low standards and we ignore all kinds of moral degradation and criminal activity, but we draw the line with human trafficking.

"Our contractors are discreet and complete their missions, but they keep their eyes open to circumstances that might void our relationship with the client. It helps negotiations should we continue providing services and, in cases like this, provides us with a breach-of-contract that allows us to walk away early without sacrificing our completion bonus. Stan alerted us to a situation where a young girl (introduced as the VIP's niece) was taken onto Dr. Talgat Kozhaev's private jet at Manassas Airport outside of Washington, D.C. There was little actionable data, but he captured several photos. The girl is Carmen Lucia Sánchez. This is the last of three pictures known to exist. Her mother presented one to the Honduran authorities after she went missing. Customs and Border Protection took another at the Mexican border and Stan took this one a week later."

Gradually, the image of a girl, no older than ten, materialized on the screen. Julian's heart sank. Memories of Emily being that age seemed like a distant echo from the past. He couldn't conceive the fear and confusion that must have gone through the little girl's head as they moved her from place to place.

"We tracked the plane to Algerian airspace, and then all airborne identification indicators went blank. We provided the information to every government agency who would listen to us. At first, Homeland Security and the State Department appeared interested, but our follow-up calls came to nothing. As soon as we brought up Dr. Talgat Kozhaev's name a second time, we were told, 'We'll do everything we can.' Frustrated by the bureaucratic dismissal, we increased our efforts and pressed on with our own investigation."

At that moment, Julian knew it didn't matter what Val did or said next. It didn't matter that he had been kidnapped and held as a comfortable captive. Regardless of how he got to this point, he was determined to stay and do whatever it took to rescue Carmen and anyone else from the clutches of Dr. Talgat Kozhaev. Reflecting on Demitri's earlier comment about coming for the money and staying for the revolution, Julian thought that, ultimately, he was here to stay for the victory, especially if it meant helping children gain their freedom.

"Carry on Demetri," Val said.

Drone footage streamed across the screen, at first similar to the appearance of a TV nature series with clear, vibrant images of mountains and valleys, but then moved in closer, looking like a high-budget documentary showing a mountaintop palace of the rich and famous. It looked like an intricate sandcastle, a medieval design, with two domed rooftops and matching guard towers. However, the image's most captivating feature was undoubtedly the sheer cliff that plunged a thousand feet to one side, revealing a village below that bore an uncanny resemblance to a Star Wars movie set, reminiscent of Tatooine. On the other side of the palace, the land dropped away slowly, and the arid higher elevations gave way to bushes and trees in colors from yellow to green, as if Autumn's approach depended entirely on elevation. Water ran off the snow-capped peaks, creeks forming rivers draining into a large lake in the lush valley.

Demetri spoke in a low serious tone, "The Kozhaev lineage has owned this palace for centuries, though they never truly called it home. Its remote location rendered it impractical until the age of helicopters simplified visits and resupply. When the mainstream medical community dismissed Kozhaev's research, he saw in this age-old estate the isolation he craved to pursue his work. He carved a runway into the hillside, set up a hydroelectric system, and fortified the place with advanced surveillance and robust fencing. The flurry of activity didn't go unnoticed. Five-Eyes, the International Intelligence Alliance, redirected a satellite to monitor the site. Even GRU, Russia's military intelligence, dispatched operatives to investigate. Eventually, they concluded it was merely the ambitious project of a man rooted in a history of deep-seated paranoia, and they let him construct his secluded stronghold."

A series of grainy, still photographs, most of them taken through telephoto lenses, showed children playing on an elaborate play structure. "We estimate that in the past two years they have flown over a thousand children into the compound. Rumors swirled—some believed it was a school for the gifted, while others thought it was a refuge for the terminally ill. Today, we're certain of its purpose. These children are treated no better than living petri dishes. They serve as in vivo hosts, producing the blood and serum Kozhaev sells to his client list. Their youthful bodies are the very infrastructure Kozhaev relies upon for his niche concoctions. Many in high places believe he's pioneering life extension techniques, and they're all too willing to overlook the stark human cost. Each month, Kozhaev makes his rounds, circling the globe, catering to these elites. Afterward, he retreats to his secluded mountain lab, profiting in ways only the darkest forces could appreciate.

"With each passing month, Kozhaev becomes increasingly indispensable to those sculpting the new world order. His dominion stretches further, his authority strengthens, and his coffers swell. We've reached out for cooperation with government bodies worldwide. Yet, none are casting even a wary eye his way, let alone making efforts to curb his activities."

"Our initial push to bring him to justice has made *us* the hunted. Genesis Security now finds itself ostracized in both D.C. and London." Demitri took a deep breath, straightened his back and continued, "We're determined to resist this impending shift in global dynamics or, at the very least, curtail this agent of chaos. In this crusade, we are alone. And Val? She remains fiercely dedicated to shielding these children from Kozhaev's looming shadow."

Val raised from her chair with the ease of someone more used to standing than sitting. She looked pleased as she walked to Demitri, kissed him on the cheek and showed she was ready to take over the briefing. "Thank you. Your work on this operation has been amazing, and I commend you."

Demitri retrieved his glass of water and took his seat as the robotic arm retracted into the wall. Julian noticed Marco pressed into his chair with an unease that said he knew nothing about any of this.

Val made eye contact with Marco. "I am sorry to keep this a secret from you and Justin. I know you have realized the pressure has been building around here, but I've had my reasons for leaving you both out of the loop. One of them is that I've needed you to stay on your tasks and not be distracted.

"Losing even one operative is devastating enough, but while chasing Kozhaev, we lost four excellent soldiers and a young woman—an innocent contractor. We have endured this mission in silence, constantly hoping for good news. Initially, we faced only disappointment, but now we have new information that may offer some hope—if we all work together.

"Julian, before I go on, I want to know if I can count on you for this operation. The offer for the forced vacation in the Philippines is still open, but now you know the entirety of our cause. What is your decision?"

He had already decided, but this was the first time he was asked for a public commitment. It was Julian's moment to declare his stance, a symbolic baptism of sorts. He wasn't prepared, but he got up and turned to face the others. "Since my wife Faith died, I've been lost. To say I've lacked purpose is an understatement. The only reason I've put up with all the state requirements and pointless laws regulating every inch of my existence is because I love my daughter and grandson. For a long time now, I thought God just left me to be sad and ineffective. Maybe that is part of the desert he needed me to go through, or maybe I'm just blind and didn't realize I might still have something to contribute."

He felt the hairs on the back of his neck tingle and he opened his hands outward, beamed with elation and felt twenty years younger, "Without a doubt, I'm with you." He pivoted to face Val, his eyes alight with determination. "This is a hill I'm willing to die on."

She walked over and embraced him. As the others applauded, Julian knew he had joined a team working to make the world better. The cause was commendable, and that was a pleasant thought, but the deep, inner glow he felt was something much more significant—more meaningful. He realized this as he came to terms with the fact that God had more work for him to accomplish. Self-pity had been his course, and, while he knew it to be destructive, he had wallowed in it. However, this new direction gave him a purpose outside of his sadness and made him realize he was not ready to give up.

Settling back into his seat, Julian felt a profound shift within himself. While this transformation warranted deep reflection later, for now, his focus was solely on Val. She returned to her chair and she faced her team.

"Thank you, Julian. You might never fully grasp what this means to our efforts, but I'm immensely grateful that you're on board. While you may not yet have a complete understanding of why your skills are vital to our success, as I delve into our recent failure, everything will become clear."

Chapter 19

VAL POSITIONED HERSELF BESIDE the presentation wall, effortlessly engaging her audience. Her smile, warm and welcoming, shifted into a serious and earnest expression. "As you know, I have no compulsion to live a strictly moral life. God is merely an artificial construct that disrupts the natural course of evolution. However, I also despise evil. You might say I have come to believe in Satan, but never God."

Dr. Talgat Kozhaev appeared in more photos, but this time he had children around him, usually one or two, but never over three. A dark-skinned girl in a delicate pillowcase dress, a boy of Asian descent wearing a Nike t-shirt, but most of the images were grainy, and the only likeness identifying them as children was their comparative size—their small legs as they walked off a yacht at night, or tiny hands reaching for the rail as they climbed the stairs to a private jet.

Evidently, this was difficult for Val. Her air of confidence evaporated before Julian's eyes and her movements stiffened. He noticed that if she were breathing, it was shallow. She turned towards the scrolling images as if paralyzed and fell silent. She let the photographs speak for themselves. Finally, after what seemed like an eternity, she squared her shoulders and carried on.

"Kozhaev might not be Satan, but he is a servant of darkness.

"Once Stan brought Carmen's situation to our attention, our investigation uncovered undeniable proof of Kozhaev's appalling practice of collecting children. At any one time, the children you see represent only a fraction of the number present within the compound." An image showed the two-dimensional view of Kozhaev's palace and the surrounding grounds. "In these government photos, it's clear that the subjects are children. The high-resolution satellite images resemble a typical playground, though they were captured a year ago. The following images show a sequence taken every five days over three weeks. Noticeably, the number of children decreases. This pattern is consistent. Each month Kozhaev's jet departed as the numbers dwindled, other aircraft came and went, and a week after his departure, the number of children had increased again by the time he returned. Like clockwork, this cycle repeated every month. However, our capability to obtain any more current surveillance data, whether public or private, vanished. We even hacked into space-station imaging, but it too yielded no results—absolutely nothing.

"If I was going to conjecture, as we began to ask too many questions, the powerful players in the world got together and virtually redacted anything to do with this man. His name went missing from all World Economic Forum web presence—even their private servers. Major corporate-sponsored media scrubbed their archives of any news articles involving Kozhaev and his connections. Government agencies around the world suddenly got amnesia whenever there was any mention of the doctor. Even diverse nations, hostile to one another, seem to agree that Dr. Talgat Kozhaev cannot be subjected to any scrutiny. The extent of such a coordinated effort, protecting the privacy of a civilian, is truly mind-boggling.

"When many people decide collectively that—there's nothing to see—I get very curious. Immediately, I gave *Stan the Bodyguard* a promotion to *Stan the Agent*. To the VIP who runs the NGO, he is the same old Stan Oberland, entrusted to keep him safe. But to me, he was the closest asset we had to Kozhaev. Six weeks ago, Stan completed his first dead drop. He stole a disk.

"Do you know how difficult it is to copy a five-and-a-quarter-inch floppy disk these days? It took us eight hours to return it to Stan. His first bit of espionage was very close to being a resounding failure, but it turned out to be the break we needed."

At the mention of a floppy disk, Julian felt like two opposing waves met in a furious collision with him standing in the middle. When the feeling receded, he realized why he was there. Not only would it be difficult to find the obsolete hardware to copy a disk popular forty years ago, but finding a person who had the chops to use that same obsolete hardware to hack data, would be equally challenging.

She turned and smiled at Julian. But while she went on talking about following up with a high-altitude flyover and how the pilot was instructed to divert course and something about a no-fly-zone, he could no longer track, and Val knew it.

"Julian, perhaps it's time for a pause. Actually, let's all take a breather. The discoveries from the floppy disk are crucial, some information cannot be hurried. A dear friend of mine insists, *the mind can only absorb what the butt can endure.* American idioms do have their charm. Am I right? We will resume in fifteen minutes." With that, Val exited the room, leaving a lingering sense of intrigue in her wake.

Chapter 20

DURING THE BREAK, JULIAN considered working on the Commodore 64 and setting up the peripherals but because of the limited time, opted for a visit to the bathroom. He refilled his water and joined the men as they returned to their seats in silence. Val returned exactly at the designated time and continued where she left off.

"We've been trying to establish why they would use old hardware. It was not obvious at first, but several encryption experts have provided us with some possibilities."

Marco slouched in his chair and spoke as if stating the obvious, "Like availability of compatible technology?"

"That's one reason," Val closed the distance between herself and Marco.

His features morphed, shifting from a somber facade to an unmistakable glint of irritation.

Speaking firmly, Val directed her words straight at Marco. "There are reasons we do things the way we do. Each of you—Justin, Demitri, and yourself—are precisely positioned in this endeavor for a purpose, performing tasks we've meticulously assigned. Believe me, each one of you is an essential part of our team. You wouldn't be here, working so closely with me, if I didn't have the utmost respect for you."

She sounded and looked sincere as she scanned the men sitting before her, but then her face hardened again. "Now may I continue, or would someone else like to add a comment?" Val held the silence uncomfortably long before she resumed.

In that drawn-out silence, Julian noticed the rhythmic rise and fall of his own breath and was glad he wasn't sitting in Marco's seat.

She strode to her captain's chair and removed a floppy disc from a compartment in the armrest. There was no need to raise it and gesture towards it to get everyone's attention, but Val used the gesture to punctuate what was to come. "What we found on the disk Stan borrowed gave us an idea of what we were dealing with. It held a history of monthly blood draws and assessment of vital signs. Initially, the data appeared unremarkable, merely comprising medical test results. However, upon closer examination by our analysts, the findings were astonishing. Six months ago the individual's data read like any typical, middle-aged American male in poor health—overweight, type-2 diabetes, high blood pressure, poor cholesterol numbers, elevated PSA, low testosterone and high inflammatory markers. However, the rate of progress observed in the anonymous client during the intervening months was incredibly rapid. Of course, this could be because of many factors, but the change fell far outside normal expectations. The most recent assessment of this same person looked like it came from a twenty-year-old Navy Seal—six months from death's doorstep to robust health.

"Demitri, please tell them what we know about the computer system."

He positioned himself against the wall opposite to Val and faced the men. "These computers are pre-Y2K, presenting compatibility issues that go beyond a two-digit designation for the year-date. They use closed source operating systems and programming languages that are foreign to everyone under fifty.

"Since online surveillance isn't keyed to filter within that sphere, data may pass by unnoticed. These systems cannot be hacked through Wi-Fi, Bluetooth or any other eavesdropping technology. Keyloggers and cloning software would have to be specially designed and physically installed into the proprietary hardware. Frankly, digital security hasn't looked in that direction for decades. The approach is so out of sync with modern technology that even modest encryption efforts render their point-to-point communications extremely secure.

"We understand their methods for coordinating data transfer and scheduling, but have not been able to compromise their system. I've wanted to share this with both of you." He looked towards Justin and Marco and said, "You'll have to trust me there was nothing you could have done to help. Our entire Russian team has been working on it for weeks and nothing." Demitri locked eyes with Julian, a mischievous smile playing on his lips, and remarked, "I welcome you, Julian. You've just fallen into my personal nightmare."

"Goodness, Demitri, are you upstaging me?" Val slapped the disk back onto the armrest and declared, "In order to expose Dr. Kozhaev, we had to break into his fortress." With a smirk playing on her lips, she continued, "If he died in the process? Well, it was a risk we were willing to take."

The screen displayed a tall, athletic girl gazing intently into the distance. She grasped the long pole and started her sprint along the runway. As she planted the pole, she timed her lift-off perfectly, launching herself high into the air. A graceful twist, her body arched, feet first over and around the bar, clearing it with inches to spare. She landed on the mat, laying on her back for a moment, then sprung up and danced away, carrying her pole.

"Larisa Ivanova was not only an architecture student at the technical university, but also their top women's pole vaulter. During last year's Kazakhstan Indoor Track and Field Championships, she attracted a tremendous amount of attention for her athleticism, beauty and brains. As we were researching the Kozhaev family, we found that the Kozhaevs invited this college junior for a private reception after the event. It turns out Larisa's hometown is that gritty little village sitting at the base of the Kozhaev palace."

A series of photographs of Larisa faded in and out until one froze on the screen. It was Larisa with Dr. Talgat Kozhaev. He had his arm around her waist, and she looked anxious.

"I paid Larisa ten thousand Euros to get into the palace and provide me with a basic floor plan." Val snapped her fingers. "She was as good as her word.

"With the team in place, they asked her if she would go back and note security. Her flourishing access to the doctor and her understanding of design made Larisa a natural spy. She became a regular at the palace, and our team leader couldn't discern whether she was falling for the doctor, or was just good at espionage. When it came time to prepare a pathway for us to storm the fortress, she exceeded all expectations. She was to mount a tiny beacon at any entrance she could compromise by leaving a door ajar or a window cracked, and then go home as she did on other evenings.

"Again, she proved to be reliable." Val hesitated. "But, that night, she was not driven back to her family's home in the village below. The team leader received a text that said, *I'm staying the night.* Larisa knew what was going on and understood she would need to hide if shooting started. But with her next text, *He's going to hurt me*, the team didn't hesitate, and they moved in."

Everyone's attention was riveted to the presentation screen where night-vision video footage played. Julian noticed that the filming was unlike anything he had seen on TV or in video games. Suppressed flashes of light punctuated the shaky, chaotic footage. The pace was too fast for Julian to follow completely, but he focused intently on Val's commentary.

"Two helicopters and ten men. There were explosions beneath the ground, and the firefight was fierce but short-lived. Two aircraft attempted to flee the scene before we secured the area—one helicopter and Kozhaev's private jet. Our man with the RPG had to choose one. He destroyed the plane while it was on the runway and the helicopter escaped. It was the right choice under the circumstances, but Kozhaev was not on the plane. In fact, they spotted him in South Sudan just two days ago."

A candid picture of Larisa Ivanova replaced the turmoil on the screen.

"Larisa died that night. They found her in an upstairs chamber hanging by her wrists over a drain. He took the time to insert a needle into the posterior tibial artery at each ankle and left her to bleed to death. By the time we got to her, she had no blood left. There was nothing that could be done."

Val wiped a tear away but continued, "He had booby-trapped the palace. The detonation was incendiary, one device for each of the sixty cells, and each cell contained two or more small charred bodies—children. The massive heat blast destroyed everything instantaneously and then the extensive ventilation system closed off and choked out the flames. It was as if the raid was simply an inconvenience for Kozhaev and he would return, sweep away the ashes, and reassemble his program."

Nobody in the room moved. The anguish on Val's face paralyzed each man, and Julian had a pang of guilt. There was nothing he could have done to prevent this catastrophe, but knowing it occurred while he was wallowing in his own sorrow grounded an edge into his soul that made him feel foolish. All the counseling in the world could not have revealed a more honorable reason for moving on after Faith's death—others were suffering more than he could imagine. This time, it was Julian who wiped away a tear.

"Along with four of our team members, they killed one hundred and twenty-three children in the inferno, but there was a survivor, a ten-year-old boy. The charge in his cell never ignited. He could not move or talk, and the super-heated air burned his skin and damaged his lungs. As the remaining team members did everything in their power to keep the boy alive, they prayed for his merciful death. They did not have to watch his suffering for long, he died before the team made it to their rendezvous.

"The autopsy told us more about what was going on than any of the other evidence we took out of the country. The boy's blood was a chemical stew. Among the drugs coursing through his vascular system were puberty blockers, erythropoietin and unnatural levels of growth hormone. It surprised them to find heavy metals in his blood, thimerosal and aluminum salts, which are notorious chemicals added as adjuvants used to elicit a higher likelihood of immune response to vaccines. But here is the most notable finding—the boy had been treated with gene therapy modalities. Not just one, like the spike protein found in the COVID mRNA jab, but dozens. His body literally had become a genetically modified organism.

"The doctors said he would not have lived even without the injuries. A red blood cell can live for one hundred and twenty days. Due to the condition of his blood, he only had a couple weeks at most and each day would be agonizing.

"It will not surprise you to learn that our team cataloged a crematorium next to the palace. There was no detonation in that building, but the oven was hot. I realize this is difficult to hear, but it doesn't take a highly trained intelligence analyst to figure out what is going on. Dr. Talgat Kozhaev has been stealing children, poisoning their bodies to produce anti-aging and life-extending agents he then provides to some of the richest and most powerful people in the world. Any process where children are exploited like expendable lab rats, mercilessly discarded once their utility wanes, must be crushed."

An empty screen during Val's last explanation left Julian's imagination up to creating the images. While he was glad not to see experiments on children or their charred bodies, his mind raced to equally offensive visions. He felt an overwhelming heaviness, as if an extra measure of gravity bound him to his seat. A water glass sat inches away from his hand, and his mouth felt dry as the desert, but an immense weight would not allow him to even lift an arm. He sat there like the others, looking catatonic on the outside, but his mind spiraling out of control, preparing for what Val would say next.

Navigating her way between Julian and the now-blank screen her voice eased into acquiescence. "Each of us is here for our own reasons. Demitri grew up in Russia, a confused country—impressive leadership, but no soul. Marco fell out of a death cult, a splinter group of ANTIFA. We caught him and offered a future. Justin came to us as Jostan." She whispered in Arabic then continued, "Thanks to Pavel, he found people who would encourage his genius and he became part of a family—eccentric, but family just the same.

"Now you—Julian. As you made clear, I brought you here against your will, but you're staying for a higher, divine purpose. You see, the world is not out of control. It is simply being controlled by evil people and administered by fools."

Val lifted her hands and half-spun as she backed away. No photograph or raw video footage streamed on the screen behind her, but a hint of a colorful backdrop appeared—matching her movements as if a choreographed dance. But when she froze in place, intent on Julian's eyes, a barely perceivable glow pulsated in subtle tones around her. The wall behind her disappeared, as did the ceiling above, and the floor too was gone. Val hovered in a timeless toric shaped aura.

Her laugh felt intimate, like an agreement between friends, and faded with her saying, "I pulled all of you from the sea and plied you with dreams of liberty. Julian more literally than the rest, but I digress. Many have died for such a cause, and not in vain. I understand a glimpse of what moves each of you. But I wonder as virtue collides right here, right now—will it be the children... after all?"

Chapter 21

"Wow, four hours and twenty-three minutes? And you look like you just started," Marco said with a chuckle, casually flipping his phone in his hand before calling Demitri. "He'll be a bear until he shakes off his beauty-sleep, but he'll know what to do next. If it were me, I'd wait until the sun comes up before I'd disturb Val, but hey, it's not my call, and there is a lot riding on this operation."

This is a place Julian had visited ever since he got his first PC. Hacking, while a singular thrill, came mixed with disappointment. Like all his other breakthroughs, this successful night left him in an emotional downward spiral—drained of life, but happy to be living. He found that the best, or at least the most harmless remedy, was to indulge in carb-heavy snacks and a Red Bull. Then, immerse himself in multiplayer video games, with chess as another suitable alternative. Marco readily supported Julian's post-hacking recovery and set up a chessboard, choosing white for himself and making the first move.

When Demitri entered The Ballast, the white and black pieces struggled in an intense battle for supremacy, while the two programmers smiled like they were having the time of their lives.

"What's so urgent that you dragged me out of bed? It's impossible you've cracked it this fast. So, what's up? And why are you wasting time playing chess?" Demitri inquired, with a mix of disbelief and curiosity.

"Look," Marco said, pointing to Julian's workstation.

Demitri studied the screen carefully, scrolled up and then down again and muttered, "Holy shit."

As Marco advanced a white pawn and leaned back, Justin entered the room and went right to the chessboard and examined it carefully.

"Come here and see this," Demitri told Justin in a near growl.

Justin was forced to tear himself away from the chess game to see what Julian had done that was worthy of Demitri's unusual mood.

Demitri stood up and said, "It's time to stop playing." He walked over to the kiosk, dropped a tea bag into his mug and filled it with hot water. "Clearly, this looks like solid work, but I need you to walk me through your process. It would be best if you keep moving forward and explain what you're doing. Repeating this process for a second time should be faster, unless you just stumbled onto this by accident." Demitri's voice showed some skepticism as he said, "I've seen people fall into a hack by mistake more than once. I don't want to doubt you, but I just don't see how you could have pulled this off—so quickly—and without sleep."

Julian hated tearing himself away from the chessboard, his brain had not recovered from the exuberant letdown of hacking into a novel computer system. Uncovering a file full of details about one of Kozhaev's clients had been an emotional high, but reduced his ability to resume that level of concentration. He skidded along muddy mental pathways which gave little traction. The others were watching a duplicate of Julian's screens on their own monitors, the digital equivalent of looking over his shoulder—it made him self conscious. He needed to reacquire the lost momentum, but found getting back into the process more tedious than he expected.

Demitri literally stood over his shoulder and watched every keystroke. For more than a few minutes, Julian wondered if maybe he did simply stumble over the path to success. He agonized through an opaque fog, feeling his way along a rut that he couldn't be sure even existed.

"I've got it!" Justin burst out.

Heads turned in unison towards him, including Julian's, as if a momentous discovery had just been made, their eyes reflecting a mixture of expectation and admiration for the young prodigy. But he stared back, with an expression that barely acknowledged any encouragement at all. In fact, he appeared embarrassed.

"What do you *got*?" Demetri asked.

"Sorry, I got nothing. Well, something..." Justin motioned towards the chessboard with a lame grin. "I figured out how Julian can beat Marco in three moves."

Marco threw a half eaten chicken wrap. Justin held up his hand to block the projectile, but only made things worse when its contents unwrapped before hitting him.

"Enough! If you two can't handle the gravity of our task, perhaps ping-pong is more your speed. You're just a distraction here," Demitri said.

"That's it!" exclaimed Julian, suddenly envisioning the three moves required to checkmate Marco's king. He didn't need Justin's help, just the assurance that it was possible. As understanding emerged, he smiled. Justin's revelation caused another unintended illumination—a fresh path in Julian's mind, guiding him to the piece of code essential for repeating his previous breakthrough. With his subconscious unburdened, the route to his hack became clear, and he started typing, capitalizing on his euphoric state of flow.

The energy in the room became palpable as the team puzzled through the developing source code. Any action that he took which was not understood, became a question. Someone would ask for a clarification of an abstraction, method, or a process, and just as often, Julian volunteered a specific tactic of his cyber attack on an unwitting foe. But, mostly, the process resembled an operating theater and the *interns* simply watched and tried to learn.

Time lost all meaning and they pushed on like that without a break until Julian pumped his fist in the air and exclaimed, "Got you!"

"How long was that?" Demitri asked, then answered his own question "Damn! Two hours and eight minutes."

"It's legit," Marco confirmed, his voice a mix of surprise and admiration. "He's unearthed another one of Kozhaev's clients."

"I've never seen anything as elegant as that!" Justin beamed with excitement. "It took me a while to figure out, but I understand what Julian just did, and his strategy is flawless. Give Marco and me a day and we can write code to automate this."

"We'll have every contact, client and supplier who uses this network," Marco added. "It's as if Julian discovered Dr. Evil's rolodex."

"This looks promising, but there's a possibility this represents low hanging fruit. It might not be this easy every time. However, if we can scale this and amp it up, we'll have total control of their information before they can send a warning memo to fix the bug," Demitri said. "It's time to wake-up Val."

Chapter 22

JULIAN AWOKE TO THE faint sound of voices, their words just out of reach. Initially, he mistook it for a perplexing dream. However, as the fog of sleep lifted, he recognized the voices as Val's and Justin's and they were speaking in Arabic.

As his memories slowly returned, Julian remembered Val being informed of his success and her insistence that he get some much deserved rest. His rest was now interrupted, but before stirring or opening his eyes, he overheard Justin switch to English and say, "Maybe we should let him sleep."

Val answered, "He's been out for six hours, and we need him. You and Demitri are close, but you're missing something that only Julian can figure out. Wake him up!"

"I'm awake," Julian said as he propped himself onto an arm. "What's the problem?" He stared at the two dim figures in his room. "Haven't you ever heard of knocking?"

"We knocked—for three solid minutes," Justin said.

"Since this is my boat, and you are just a guest, I breached the door to make sure you were alright," Val said.

"You breached the door?"

"Well, I used the housekeeping override."

"Okay. Whatever. What's going on?" Julian asked.

"This is going to be a long day. Take a shower and meet us in the dining room. Marco is at his limit and needs to get some sleep.

Demitri is bleary-eyed and needs to unwind and Justin is famished."
She placed her hand on Justin's head and tousled his hair. "I want to
get everyone together for a meal. We need to decompress as a team
and I can think of no better way to do that than a little relaxation
around food.

"Plus there is the matter of Dr. Kozhaev's clients. The ones you
found by hacking into his database."

"What about them?"

"They have been murdered," Val said as she and Justin left his
room and closed the door behind them.

"How do you know they're dead?"

"Well, you are looking spry. Thank you for joining us." Val said
from the head of the table. Demitri sat to her right, Justin and Marco
on her left, leaving two empty seats.

"Have a mimosa, the orange juice is freshly squeezed."

Cedric sat a tall slender champagne glass on the table identifying
where Julian should sit down.

"I loathe business talk at the table, especially when it involves dead
bodies. Do you mind terribly? We know so little about the people
in our lives. Truly, Julian, we know you are an extraordinary hacker,
but what is your favorite color?"

"Blue," he said absently.

"The chef has outdone herself. The food is magnificent." Val
motioned for him to help himself to the family style arrangement of
dishes and platters centered along the middle of the table. Val lifted
her eyes and proclaimed, "Ah, and our honored guest returns."

Julian joined the rest of the table in watching as a woman
in her early fifties approached with confident steps. If she had

on makeup, it was minimal, and her short wheat-colored hair did nothing to soften her aggressive appearance. She did not look angry but appeared to be the antithesis of Val's curious effervescence and enduring femininity. He pegged this woman for a cop or security. Even her clothing, while civilian, had paramilitary characteristics—navy-blue slacks and a pale button-down blouse. While form-fitting at the shoulders and chest, it hung loose enough at the waist to allow her to conceal a pistol.

"Megan, this is the man who has cracked open our case, Julian Comstock. Julian, I'd like you to meet Megan Ward. She oversees the branch of Genesis Security that is spearheading this entire operation. You might say, you find them virtually, and her people follow up personally."

Julian shook her hand and immediately regretted not anticipating the intense grip. Megan then took her seat at the end of the table, opposite Val.

"You missed the chef's wonderful description of what she prepared for us. Let me see if I can recall. *Wild-caught, local salmon seasoned and pan-seared*—I should add that it is perfection—*with a drizzle of lemon-dill sauce.*" She removed a silver lid from a platter and said, "*Accompanied by roasted fingerling potatoes and sauteed asparagus.*" Val slid the platter to Demitri to pass along.

With a broad smile, Marco slid a bottle of wine across the table. "Here, Julian," he urged, gesturing towards the glasses. "Pour some for both of you." His eyes flicked towards Megan with a nod, the corners crinkling with genuine enthusiasm. "Woodward Canyon, Sauvignon Blanc. I believe you'll find it quite to your liking. Recently, I can't seem to get enough of it."

Val gave Marco a disapproving look that everybody seemed to notice except Marco. "Megan, I have found it fascinating to inquire about peoples' favorites. For instance, may I ask, *what is your favorite color?*"

"Teal. But I seem to be at a disadvantage. Did I come in at the end of the icebreaker?"

"Of course, forgive me. Marco says orange is his favorite, Demitri, Julian and Justin share blue and mine is Vermilion. I find it so amusing to listen to the answers to this question. Nine out of ten men will answer with a basic color, but over half of all women choose nuanced colors. I would be shocked if ever the tide changes and men choose crimson, saffron and cyan, while women pick red, yellow and blue. But, what inevitably causes me to laugh, is the consistency of my experiment. We are so predictable within our freedom of choice."

Val placed her napkin on the table. "You must excuse me. I have an appointment with the captain regarding shifting *Elysium Prime* to another port. We have had time to delight in what the chef has prepared, but Julian, there is plenty of food. You and Megan should get to know each other." She rose and left the room without another word.

Demitri stood up. "That was a fantastic meal, and the company has been terrific, but I've got a ton of work to do. Justin, please join me. They each assumed stations on either side of Marco and began to raise him from his seat. "Marco, I want to thank you for staying up all night with Julian and working hard all morning with the rest of us. Now, it is time for you to get some sleep."

Justin grabbed Marco's hand before he could seize the bottle of wine. The three men walked off together, leaving Julian and Megan Ward alone at the table.

"Did I miss a cue to leave?" Julian inquired, slightly puzzled.

"No, Julian. I asked Val if she would arrange some time for us to be alone. I need some answers," Megan Ward said. "I'll be direct. I don't trust you. In fact, I suspect you are a mole."

Julian didn't have time to recoil from his shock before she went on in an accusing tone.

"I value the opinion of Val and Demitri very much and they assure me you could not have possibly betrayed the names of Kozhaev's clients. Val says you are a genuine believer in the cause of freedom and Demitri informs me you had little opportunity to reveal the names. But I still need to know how this evil syndicate of child-stealing bastards found out exactly which two men you identified during your cyber attack."

"I do not know what you are talking about," Julian said.

"Maybe you don't. But I intend to know for sure, before I decide."

Megan stood, placing her fists against the high-gloss wood surface and leaned her body inward. "Genesis Security employs world-class hackers. We've spent weeks trying to execute a cyber attack. Then, you join us and hack into their database in a matter of hours. You reveal detailed information regarding a client of Kozhaev, then in half the time, you identify another.

"You revealed two hot prospects who we had hoped could lead us to the ringleaders—with the promise of more to come. We activated a private investigator in Cape Town, South Africa for the first man and another in London for the second. The private investigator in Cape Town found his man at the morgue. And when the London PI reported, his man was dead on arrival at the hospital. Do you know how they died?"

"How would I know that? Apparently, I was sleeping through it," Julian said.

"Both men died from exsanguination."

"I don't know what that means."

"Exsanguination is death from the loss of blood. Their entire vascular system was drained—all their blood, gone. But that is only a morbid curiosity. How did they find out that you had identified someone as a client of Dr. Kozhaev?"

"I have no clue. I need to go back to The Ballast and figure this out."

"My investigation is ongoing. You and I are having this little meet-up because two men are dead, and they're of no use to me now. So, there's no need to rush things. I'm going to find out if you communicated to our enemies, or if this is just an awful coincidence. Either way, I've got to make sure the next person we track down in Kozhaev's club isn't taken out before we get to them.

"I want you to go back to your stateroom and think this through. Cedric will see you to your room. Our security protocols require that your door be locked. If you have any insights that may help, use the intercom."

Chapter 23

"I KNOW WHAT HAPPENED! I need to get to The Ballast, and I need everybody there." Nobody confirmed his message through the intercom, but seconds later Cedric opened the door with a broad smile. "Didn't I tell you your life will never be the same?" as he ushered Julian out of his room.

Demitri and Justin were at their workstations. Marco's computer was dark, and Val was not there. Megan Ward sat in a corner, staring at him. "I think I figured this out, but I need help." He sat down at the Commodore 64 and said, "I'm going to move through this slowly so you can keep up. It's important that I don't make a mistake at this juncture. There will be points of entry into their system that, if I'm not very cautious, could trigger an alert and ruin anything we hope to achieve. Can I get a camera to record this? If things go bad, I want to review everything, and if this works, it will help the documentation."

"Haven't you heard our surveillance is omnipresent?" Demitri said, as he pointed to the ceiling and then motioned to several other locations throughout the room.

Julian looked up and saw a tiny little camera looking down on him. "Okay, good."

An hour later, Demitri ordered, "Don't do that! Push your keyboard away so I can see your hands."

Julian felt a surge of intense pain ripple through his body as his muscles locked up in uncontrollable spasms. He lay disoriented and helpless on the floor.

"Don't move a muscle, or I'll put you through that again," a woman's voice shouted.

His mind felt scrambled and his body writhed useless. A jolt of realization hit him as sharply as the initial shock from the Taser—it was Megan Ward who had sent the barbed probes into his back.

"Demitri, put him in cuffs. If he gets loose, I will not hesitate to shoot him." Megan Ward insisted.

Julian didn't know if she meant *shoot* as in—activate the Taser again—or *shoot* as in the lead variety. All he could think of was Justin-the-prophet telling him about being tased, and that the ship had a large freezer. He didn't want to die.

The windowless room was small with a bright light, but no naked bulb like the interrogation rooms in the movies. Even with his hands cuffed behind him and the hard, cold steel of the straight-backed chair pressing into him, Julian realized his thoughts of torture and execution were overly dramatic. Still, he had to admit, everything he had experienced recently, presented more than enough evidence that dramatic events had become part of his life. He wondered, *who could say what might happen next?* and prayed for understanding.

The door behind him swung open, and he felt a pair of arms wrap around him in a quick hug. Val glided around him until she knelt at his feet, looking into his eyes. Julian breathed in deep, relaxing into the moment and her presence, thankful for the diversion.

"Oh, Julian," Val said. "I'm so sorry. Megan insists on reviewing all the videos before considering your release. Demitri explained the whole situation to her, but she remains wary of everyone. It turns out, he simply couldn't see what you were doing. Your hands obstructed his view, and he lost track of your keystrokes. Demitri just wanted you to move your hands for better visibility. Unfortunately, Megan misinterpreted his request and assumed you were involved in sabotage, so she didn't hesitate to tase you. Despite a full explanation, she remains suspicious and believes there's something sinister at play."

Val grew quiet and her apologetic gaze left him as she stared into the monochromatic wall in front of them. She slid down further and sat on the floor, hooked an arm over his knees and leaned her torso against his legs. They did not speak for several minutes as they waited together in the gentle hush.

Again, the door opened. Val got up from the floor, a quick blush of embarrassment on her face. With no other chair in the room except the one he was tied to, it had made sense for her to sit at his feet, a mix of practicality and kindness. But, as Demitri walked in, Val's slightly self-conscious manner showed an unexpected side of her.

Demitri slapped a hand on Julian's shoulder and said, "Sorry, old man, I owe you one. But before I take these cuffs off, I want to know there are no hard feelings. Even though I think I could take a punch from you without a problem, I'd rather we be friends."

"Just take them off and we'll find out."

Chapter 24

AT FIRST, HIS BODY and his mind didn't seem to connect. Being tased had shaken him to the core of his being. Although the pain had quickly subsided, its memory lingered so closely that he found himself inadvertently constricting his muscles and holding his breath. Julian had been eager to rejoin the others—he had work to do. It seemed sensible that keeping busy would be the best thing for his lingering apprehension, so picking up where he left off made perfect sense. But he wasn't ready for the onslaught of emotion which coursed like lightning through him as he entered The Ballast. It didn't go as planned, not because of the task at hand, but because Megan Ward sat smugly by the door.

Fury chose the same path as the electricity from the Taser, only this time it empowered him. Julian's words came out in a harsh growl, tinged with a raw edge he hardly recognized. "I've never laid a hand on a woman, but I swear, if she doesn't leave this boat immediately, one of us is going to die!" Never had he felt the urge to release such a menacing rage, but with Megan Ward in front of his face—he lost control.

Demitri inserted himself between the two, ushering Megan away with no altercation. Once she was gone, he said, "Don't worry, she was just waiting for the chopper to return. She'll be off this ship in a few minutes." His voice slowed and he asked, "Now, where would you like to pick up with this clever hack of yours?"

Again, Julian held his breath and all his muscles tensed, but this time the thought of getting into his work made him cycle his breathing and relax. He looked up into Demitri's sincere eyes. "Right where we left off. I've got an idea, and I think we can crush this."

Justin, Demitri and Julian established a smooth workflow among themselves. Marco had rested, shaking off his fatigue, and rejoined the group in a sober state. He displayed a more humble side, almost contrite, demonstrating a willingness to assist.

Even though clocks hung on the walls and appeared on every screen, time became inconsequential. Half-eaten sandwiches, still in their wrappers, littered the space. Occasionally, Val peeked her head in and asked if they needed anything, but she must have finally gone off to bed because her visits stopped. Eventually, the room's energy dwindled as well.

As hope of a quick, simple programming solution waned, Julian wondered if it would be better to tell everyone to stop. Marco was the only programmer who didn't seem tired, but he had also become sullen. Perpetual frustration over time had derailed their momentum. Maybe calling it quits would allow for rest and recovery, but Julian doubted he would be able to sleep.

What started as sensible audacity had transformed into doubts as the minutes ticked by without progress. His idea was grandiose—they would write code to not only infiltrate, but also take over the old-fashioned, self-hosted bulletin board scheme and capture the entire network with a brute force attack. All the data, every account, each transaction, and all correspondence would be theirs. Kozhaev's syndicate would be totally exposed. Once the data was in their hands, they would have the time they needed to break the encryption with no one pulling the plug in retaliation.

Demitri wrote some words on the whiteboard in Cyrillic letters. When asked, he said, "All or nothing!" Justin wrote the equivalent in Arabic. Noticing the lack of English, Julian spelled out "All or nothing!" Marco grabbed the marker and added, "Ride or Die," bringing a few laughs. But hours later, as hope was fading, Marco raised his voice as if to summon any remaining resolve, "Rockets explode until the developers get it right. It's just the way it goes."

"You're right, but test rockets don't get people killed," Demitri reminded him.

Marco responded, "Don't you think we should remember that those dead men represent the worst of humanity? I mean sacrificing children to use their blood. Those men deserved to die."

"Guys!" Julian interrupted, "Marco, we're not rocket scientists. Demitri, I don't want to step on your toes, but you got me tased, so now you owe me. Plus, I'm the oldest here." He stood and backed away from his workstation. "Let's take a break. Nobody works for the next sixty minutes. Take a power nap, get some fresh air, eat something, have a beer, play Polytopia for all I care. Just come back in sixty minutes, and we'll take a vote. As I see it, we have two choices. We can decide to push onward, maybe we can break through this fog before the sun comes up, or we turn in, get the rest we need and hit it tomorrow." Julian didn't wait for a consensus. He walked out of The Ballast, letting the door close behind him.

"Maybe some fresh air?" Val's voice sounded soft, as if coming from far away.

Julian turned to her. She looked small, curled up on one of the huge couches, across the expanse of the room near to the grand piano. She stood, yawned and stretched, then slowly made her way in Julian's direction. Val wore a gray cashmere turtleneck and white, wide-leg pants. Her braided hair fell to the front of her right shoulder.

"I didn't even realize we left the dock. Where are we going?" Julian asked.

"Seattle. Where else?" Val said.

"You're taking me home?"

"It is not about you. Our reasons vary widely. We have business there—an appointment with Volvo—our diesel engines require attention. Megan Ward is setting up a new branch of Genesis Security, and I feel Seattle has potential. Bankers aren't the only ones who buy when there is blood in the streets. Fortunately, there is no blood on the top floor of a building with a helipad we hope to use as our Pacific Northwest headquarters. Also, I promised the young men a night out. Justin turned twenty-one while we were at sea, and he is keen to drink legally in your country. He has been around the world and has been of drinking age for years, but your country is full of... oddities. A child, not even a teenager, can determine that they are not the right sex, and receive drugs and surgeries altering their very nature, yet half the college students cannot even buy a drink."

The perplexed look left her face to be replaced with an accepting smile. "So you see, there is more to life than righting wrongs, preserving liberty and saving children. Life moves on, and sometimes we simply need to get out of the way so others can live theirs. And, yes, if you wish, you may leave us and go to your home, but I had hoped you would like to stay aboard with us. I do understand that your home is Seattle, where you have Emily, Asher and a lifetime of memories, but I would love to have you sign on with the *Elysium Prime.* The Ballast could use someone with your skills and maturity. The wages would be of no consequence to you given your wealth, but what we lack in employee compensation we make up tenfold in excitement."

"You want me to work for you?"

"Yes. I mean no. I don't know, Julian. You confound me, and I have little capacity for that state of mind." Val turned her head and distanced herself just a few steps before she turned back. I have been in communication with Mitch, and he has returned from his cruise of the San Juan Islands aboard your sailboat, the *Horizon's Edge*. Your floating home awaits, and knowing how fastidious Mitch is, I'm certain you will find it in excellent condition. All I can tell you is that you have options."

She walked past him and said, "Follow me." She took several more steps, turned and looked at him. "I must apologize for my indomitable will. I am used to directing people, and they follow. Forgive me. I will try again." Val tilted her head downward and to the side, appearing embarrassed. Quickly regaining eye contact, she took a step towards him and spoke in a soft and hopeful tone, "Julian, I would so appreciate your company, will you join me on deck? I will ask the captain to slow our progress. From the sundeck, we can see all the stars. If we stand just aft of the stack, there is no breeze whatsoever at low speeds. It is lovely. You will see."

There was no breeze—none at all. Julian knew nothing about megayachts but found this phenomenon curious. In order to take advantage of the eddy, they needed to stand close to one another. "You're right about life moving along despite our desire to control everything. I think that is what you were getting at when we were downstairs. Learning that is something that has never come easy for me."

She stood with her arms crossed, looking into the night sky. "I don't understand men and their obsession with computers, but I believe the desire to control everything is at the heart of it. Engineering and technologies are anything but random. It must provide a sense of security to know the outcome. In a small way, if you are clever enough, you can determine your destiny. But to me, it seems to be a distraction from relationships."

"Faith would have agreed with you. She would move heaven and earth for people and cared nothing for the tools of a technological age."

"I am sorry you have lost her. She sounds like a wonderful person. I think I would have liked her very much," Val said.

They stood in silence. The water was very calm for the Puget Sound. The sky was crystal clear, stars dripping from the blackness of space and the Milky Way appeared to drift to the northwest. Julian knew exactly where they were in the universe—heading south, halfway between the southern tip of Lopez Island and the Canadian city of Victoria. However, in all the universe, he still didn't know where he wanted to go.

"Julian, do not take this wrong." She turned around, took small steps and moved into him until her back rested against his chest and she leaned her head against his shoulder.

He said, "Don't take this wrong," as he wrapped his arms around her, and there they nestled together gazing at the same stars.

In time, Julian's legs were getting tired, and his mind ran in a different direction for each constellation he picked out. "You know what you said about distraction?"

"I'm not sure I do," Val said in a sleepy voice.

He dropped his arms from around her. "You know—men get distracted by technology?"

She rocked away from him and turned to look into his face. "Don't tell me you're thinking about technology," she teased, lightly tapping his chest. "Why do men always prove my point?"

"I've got it! Can you get everybody together in The Ballast? Announce 'all-hands' through the intercom, or 'sound the klaxon' or something!" Julian said excitedly.

"Yes! I'll have your team meet you right away." Her smartwatch glowed and she said, "I've got this. Run along."

Chapter 25

"Yes!" Marco burst out. "It was right under our noses. How many times did we map the server? It just looked like an unused port. But now we've got them."

There were excited looks and high fives around the room, but Val didn't show any exuberance, and Julian realized he had not taken the time to explain his breakthrough. "I'll stay out of the weeds, but basically, Marco just found a port that they are using for a tape backup system. They're committed to this idea of old technology, so it makes sense. It's rare today, but it's a smart way of controlling their data flow. They get to micromanage the entire database and exclude outsiders in a variety of ways. But what made little sense to me was that speed and memory limitations would also eliminate their capacity to scale and maintain anything that got too complicated. There is a reason we use computers with modern processors and storage—we need the capacity which can handle the data. From what we've discovered, we are dealing with a major international syndicate. They must have a way to deal with a large amount of data, but we see no evidence of it. So how are they keeping up?"

Val sat down and crossed her legs at the ankles. Her posture was perfect and she maintained a sincere expression as she concentrated. Julian understood Val had become his pupil and he needed to be a more effective professor so he tried a different approach. "You've been to a vineyard. How are the vines watered?"

"Drip irrigation."

"Exactly. Each vine receives water from small emitters. Picture these emitters as Commodore 64 computers, with water representing data. Unlike water, though, data flows in both directions. Like dripping water for a plant. It's a slow process, but over time, it does the job. Now, let me ask you a question. How much water is available in the vineyards you've seen?"

"Why, there is always as much as is required to grow the vines and produce the grapes," Val said.

"Yes. And with our computer example, a Commodore 64, the emitter, can only provide for one vine at a time. During our search for a data lake, or in our example a water reservoir, we never found a source. We scoured the system, but there was nothing. While being broken up into isolated emitters makes it very secure, it makes no sense. It can grow a vine but not nourish an entire vineyard—yet the vineyard exists.

"We cannot see the reservoir, but because there are many living vines we must deduce it exists. My earlier hack came upon a lone emitter. I exploited that, and we found just one of Dr. Kozhaev's clients—a single vine. Then I found the second—another single vine. What I couldn't find is any way to get to the reservoir and discover the source. That's the moment it came to me. They can turn the flow of water in the vineyard off and on at the source—the reservoir. That, too, is a very old computer strategy that hasn't been preferred for decades, but lends itself perfectly to this application—a tape backup system. They are slow, very slow, but they can handle as much data as there is tape to record it on. Since it is a gated connection, no one has access to a potentially vast reservoir of data, until it is opened."

"I follow you, but don't see how that knowledge is particularly helpful. They are not likely to open the valve and let you in to steal their data," Val said.

"Of course not, but I have hacked these before, and I can do it again. You just need to know how to knock on the door and say *pretty-please*." Julian scanned the room and found everyone looking at him. Demitri smiled, Marco looked excited, and Justin—a bit bewildered. "I know how to do this, but I need a distraction, and Justin is the man for the job."

Justin spoke up saying, "I never even heard of a tape backup system before."

"Maybe not, but you are the one that is closest to understanding how I found the two men. I'll be right here if you get stuck, but I need you to take the next few hours and look for more clients of Kozhaev's," Julian said.

"Another dead body drained of blood coming right up!" Justin said, seething with sarcasm.

Val set her gaze on Julian and her brow furrowed as she pondered out loud, "Regarding those two men... it's baffling how they became targets so swiftly after your discovery. Their elimination makes sense. After all, dead men tell no tales. But the pressing question is how did our adversaries pinpoint who you had uncovered? That very conundrum is why Megan suspected you as a mole, and it's still unanswered."

Demitri spoke up, "There are several possibilities, but with the information we have, there is no way to be sure. What we know is that Kozhaev's syndicate will need to spend their resources counteracting what it is we are doing. So the more attacks we make on their resources, the better our chances. Using the vineyard example, a worker would have to walk the rows and check each emitter to find the ones that have been compromised. There can only be a finite number of workers. We are going to keep them busy while Julian waltzes right up to the reservoir and jumps right in."

She appeared irritated and asked Demitri, "How do you know they won't just kill the people we find?"

"You're right. Two men are dead and it's likely they will continue to deal with their additional loose ends in the same way. At least until we discover someone who is too important to their operation to kill. The two murdered men were not big fish in the globalist agenda, they simply had money to spend on Kozhaev's product. One was part owner of a premier soccer team and the other, a mid-level politician using the family fortune to gain local power."

"That's interesting, but it's not an answer. How could they have done that so fast?" Val asked.

"We don't know," Demitri admitted. "You're the head of an action-oriented security company that has fast response teams. Why don't you tell me?"

Val looked incredulous as she assessed Demitri. She stood up, put on a smile, and said, "We are all tired. Thank you so much for helping me understand what is going on. Your work here is of immense importance. I am going to leave you to explore the vineyard and find your tape drive." She hesitated and turned back to Julian. "Once you find your reservoir, what then?"

Julian's face lit up as if he had already discovered what he was looking for. "Imagine every drop of that water in that reservoir is available to us while the workers are out in the field checking on the emitters. They won't detect our presence because we're not removing data, just duplicating it, drop by drop or in this case—bit by bit. By the time they finish checking the emitters, we'll have mirrored their entire database without altering a single thing. We will have a copy, but they will see no change. The reservoir is as it has always been."

Her expression flitted between amazement and unbelief but finally softened. Again, speaking directly to Julian, "No matter how this turns out, I am thankful I found you."

He did not know what to say, so he stayed silent, as she quietly left the room.

Julian spoke to his team, "Okay, are there any questions?"

"Did you kiss her?" Marco teased.

"You're too young to understand," Julian laughed. "Now let's get to work. *All or Nothing!*"

As he reflected on the evening's events, he couldn't help but notice a distinct shift in Val's behavior, a transformation that might have slipped by unnoticed if Marco had not mentioned it. Her words of appreciation, once simple and direct, now carried layers of complexity and nuance, a change that surprised him.

Val's body language, always captivating, seemed to convey an unspoken message. Despite her outward composure, there was a subtle, yet discernible, reticence in her movements. Her eyes, steady and longing for understanding, never wavered as she intently listened to Julian explaining the team's strategy. The intensity of her focus was striking. He noticed her blinking more often than usual, and as she turned to walk away, there seemed to be the hint of a tear shimmering in her eye. Though unsure, he felt a sincerity in her demeanor that hadn't been present in their earlier encounters. And he thought it was odd how she hardly paid any attention to Justin and Marco. And when it came to Demitri, her usual respect had switched to a cold, almost hostile attitude.

On the deck, gazing at the stars with Val, he didn't question if he had been untrue to Faith. The evening air was chilly. When she innocently leaned into him and he responded, he felt no guilt. But now, recalling that moment troubled him. He knew dwelling on it would overwhelm him with emotions and render him useless. Julian knew he had to stop over analyzing her actions and get back into his work. So he mentally cautioned himself using Val's own words—*Julian, do not take this the wrong way.*

Fighting self-pity was a familiar war, yet now, more pressing issues demanded his attention. Deciphering Val's complexity and unraveling his own tangled emotions must wait. He had work ahead of him and needed to get back in the game. As he breathed deep and lifted his gaze, Justin and Demitri stared back at him with troubled looks while Marco suppressed laughter.

Chapter 26

"JULIAN, YOU NEED TO wake up. The meeting is about to begin," Demitri said as he gently shook his shoulder.

The last thing he remembered was pushing away his plate. It was delicious, but he recalled only getting through half of it before he had to lay his head down and close his eyes. The cleared dining table and the absence of any curious glances eased Julian's embarrassment as he sat up quickly, shaking off the grogginess without a yawn. Everyone except Marco was watching a wall-sized TV showing the perspective of someone walking along a hallway in what looked like a modern office building. Audio accompanied the video feed, but the light breathing and even quieter footsteps proved equally uninteresting.

"Here's some of my specialty coffee. High caffeine, Death Wish Dark Roast, bulletproofed—MCT and grass-fed ghee with a pinch of cinnamon," Cedric said as he placed a large handcrafted mug in front of Julian.

Then, he walked around the table, temporarily blocking the view of the screen, to wake up Marco. Cedric placed a Red Bull on the table, grabbed Marco's shoulders and shook him.

"What the hell!" Marco yelled as he recoiled.

"My job is keeping you sharp when needed, and now, you're up! Focus!" Cedric said firmly. Before he walked away, he announced, "The galley is open, but clean your own dishes."

Val did not seem to hear Marco's outburst or notice Cedric's snarky attitude. She stayed laser-focused on the screen as if something important was going to happen any second, but all Julian saw was a video stream of someone walking along a hallway approaching a set of ornate doors made of hardwood.

"What's going on?" Marco asked, as he turned to see what everybody else was looking at.

"Justin, get them up to speed. Demitri and I have to give this our full attention," Val said.

"Okay, I'll try. Not surprisingly, our cyber attack has caught someone's eye. But the crazy thing is, a person who we assume is connected to Kozhaev's syndicate has been lighting up the dark web, insisting on a meeting. We accepted the invitation and agreed to meet at a high-end lawyer's office in... Bayview?"

"It's called Bellevue," Demitri corrected. "It's like Seattle, but with standards."

Justin continued, "We have Julie Marsh on-site—the contractor Julian spotted on the doorbell camera footage." He paused. "Curious. Julie and Julian. No matter. What we are watching is her walking through the building. The feed has been pretty boring since they took her gun and knives when she went through the security checkpoint. Too bad you slept through that. She was unhappy about it and we could even hear her snarl. There. You're all up to speed."

"Is she wearing a body cam?" Marco asked.

Demitri answered, "It's her phone. Now shut up."

Julian had a slew of questions brewing in his mind. He wanted to inquire, *How did they establish contact?* and, *Shouldn't she have backup?* He was also curious if there had been any word regarding the third client of Dr. Kozhaev that they had discovered while duplicating the tape backup. Julian recalled his name was Morgan Blackwood, from Seattle, a budding politician with aspirations to secure a position as one of Washington's senators. He wondered if they had located him yet. *Was he still alive?*

However, after hearing Demitri's sharp retort, Julian opted to hold his questions. He observed the video feed, curious about its quality. The camera angle was slightly elevated and the audio only picked up the faint sound of breathing. It wasn't until Julie spoke, Julian realized she was using earbuds, which explained why her voice came through crystal-clear.

"I'm at the door to the law firm of *Johnson, Thorn and Blackwood*. Should I continue?"

Julian could not see Val's expression as she faced the video feed, but the timbre of her voice let on that she was anxious. "Julie, we don't know what to expect, but you've been in deadlier situations. Just keep the video feed going."

"Roger that."

The door opened into a spacious lobby with a desk straight ahead. A pretty blond-haired woman smiled and said something, but Julie's mic did not pick up the sound very well. She walked over to an office door, and a tall, fit man in his early fifties opened it and greeted her with a handshake.

"Thank you for coming. I'm Morgan Blackwood. I didn't get your name." The man's voice was not loud.

"You can call me Nikita."

"Nice!" Marco said.

Demitri whispered, "Marco. I agree with you, but we need silence. I've already boosted the mic on her phone and balanced the feed as much as I can—so be quiet."

"Very well, Nikita. Please have a seat."

She continued to stand.

Mr. Blackwood leaned in, and he looked right into the camera. "I see you have a phone staring at me from your breast pocket." A Hollywood perfect smile took over his face. "I'm a stickler for quality remote communications. I want the people viewing this to hear and see everything, so let's do this." He disappeared out of the frame for a second. "Now, take your phone and use your Bluetooth to connect to my cameras."

"Am I good to proceed?" Julie asked.

Demitri gave a thumbs-up gesture and nodded.

Val relayed the message, "Yes, there is no security threat in that."

A moment later, a professional video feed shone on the screen split down the middle. The left side showing Morgan Blackwood sitting at his desk and the right side showing a thirty something woman that Julian would never have recognized from the image he had discovered from his daughter's doorbell-camera. The camera had distorted her image, making her face appear unnaturally rounded and her nose ill-proportioned. A baseball cap covered her hair, adding to the odd visual effect. This undistorted video stream showed Julie Marsh to be an attractive woman with high cheekbones, an angular jaw, a perfectly normal sized nose and stylish jet black hair.

"That's better. Now you may stand if you like, but I'm just the attorney here and I've not been prepped, so I don't know how long this will take. I've blocked out for an hour. Please, you may sit."

The video showed Julie hesitating before she sat down. Demitri typed on his laptop, muted her phone's mic and then seemed to relax when Blackwood's voice came through crystal clear. The phone image popped up as a thumbnail in the corner of the split screen. Like the high-quality video, it showed Blackwood at his desk, but from a higher angle—moving slightly with each of Julie's breaths.

The lawyer studied a monitor off to one side for a minute. Then he faced Julie and said, "My client accuses your firm of a cyber attack. The damages are catastrophic and you are responsible for two deaths. However, they are reasonable and will not pursue punitive actions if you immediately agree to the following terms. Destroy the data and any copies you have. Stop all current espionage and do not engage in those activities in the future. Consider this meeting to be your Cease and Desist Order. Failure to comply with a Cease and Desist Order can cause legal penalties, including fines and imprisonment."

This time, he looked directly into the camera positioned next to Julie. "Is the reason for this meeting clear to your employers?"

"Julie, tell him, *We know your client is Dr. Talgat Kozhaev. He has no jurisdiction or authority over us, and that we are meeting here today as a courtesy only to you, Mr. Blackwood, as we are concerned for your safety.*"

Unfazed by Julie's word for word recitation, he pressed on, "Nikita, you haven't responded in a way which suggests your employers understand the gravity of the allegations, nor have you accepted our offer. I will need an answer now. Will your employers agree to the terms and ensure a full cessation of activities as directed?"

"Say nothing. Just stare him in the eye," Val said.

He referenced his monitor again. A printer quietly spit out a sheet of paper and he held it up while still sitting at his desk. The camera auto-zoomed in on it until six names were visible. One of those names was *Genesis Security.*

"How the hell could they have figured that?" Val said. "Three are names of our competitors. I've never heard of those other two."

Blackwood's expression of delight turned into a menacing grimace. "We know you represent one of these companies. It will only be a matter of time before we zero in on which one. You clearly know how influential my client is, but do you understand how much better it will be for you to cooperate?"

"Julie, say the following and just stare him down: *Mr. Blackwood, the only reason I'm here is because we are concerned for your safety.*"

Val shot a harsh refrain across the table. "There is not a single nation or law enforcement agency on that list! Could they actually be that connected to global politics, that they are confident no law enforcement agencies are looking for them? Can it be true that no governing authority in the entire world has a shred of decency?"

"Not surprised," Marco said.

Val ignored Marco's snide answer. "Julie, tell him this and get out of there: *We know everything about Dr. Kozhaev and the worldwide syndicate that sacrifices children. It's a horrifying transhuman nightmare, and we won't rest until you all face justice.*"

Julie repeated the statement perfectly, got up, and walked to the door.

"Your name is Julie Marsh," Blackwood raised his voice and continued, "formerly, Command Sergeant Major of the United States Army, serving under Colonel Megan Ward. Currently, you work for Genesis Security, privately owned by Anastasiya Valentina Volkov."

Julie stopped in her tracks, her breathing caused the phone camera to rise and fall inches from the closed door, but she did not open it.

"Do I have permission to take him out?" Julie asked.

"Do whatever you need to, but get out of there!" Val said.

The image from her phone's camera blurred with motion as she spun around. When the image steadied, they could all see the unmistakable barrel of a gun aiming directly at the lens of her camera—at Julie's chest.

Blackwood's deep voice said, "Ms. Marsh, don't do anything stupid. I know you could kill me with your bare hands, and that is precisely why I will shoot you if you do not back away from the door and sit down. Now!"

The professional cameras showed Blackwood resuming his place behind his desk and Julie returning to her chair.

"It's time we were completely candid with one another. Julie, you may not see another sunset, but it is not me who wishes you harm. I do, however, need you to allow me to continue to speak on behalf of my client.

"There will be no further negotiations or warnings. We have received your answer, and clearly we are at an impasse. Your investigation into my client's affairs is now over and you will not proceed with any actions that will directly or indirectly harm my client or any persons involved with them.

"There have already been two deaths because of your meddling. My client valued those men, and regrettably there will be one more, because of what you set in motion. However, there will not be a fourth, because if there is a fourth—there will be a million." After a brief glance at his monitor, he turned back to the camera, his eyes reflecting a newfound determination. "If any further associates of my client are revealed, you will be responsible for the detonation of a nuclear bomb."

Blackwood took a drink of water and continued, "My client controls three nuclear devices, they are small, but each is in a major city—on different continents. If you expose any more of my clients' dealings, they will not hesitate to unleash hell on earth and you will be responsible."

Once again, Blackwood studied his monitor, but only for a moment. His composed demeanor gave way to vindictiveness. "If you think you can hunt the doctor down, expose the members of our forum and stop the natural progress of evolution, you are naive. The doctor you mentioned is only one of a multitude—he is a middleman. We are ushering in a new future. You're done with your opposition. The wave has crested and anyone in our path will be crushed." Mr. Blackwood stood, walked over to the camera and the screen went dark.

Julie's phone was the only one still broadcasting, and Demitri quickly changed the feed to be viewable in a larger format.

Blackwood's voice could be heard over Julie's audio feed. "Ms. Marsh, you said you were concerned for my safety. Why?"

Julie got to her feet. "It means your name was the third man we exposed as a client of Dr. Kozhaev's. It means we know that the blood products of dying children circulate in your veins as an attempt to defy aging. We had hoped to protect you in order to expose the leaders of the syndicate."

The steadiness in Blackwood's voice disappeared as he asked, "How did the other two men die?"

"They drained out every drop of their blood," Julie said as the image showed her moving towards the door. She stepped through the doorway and past the reception desk. The camera turned briefly to show the receptionist. They heard her say, "You may want to call nine-one-one, Mr. Blackwood isn't looking at all well."

The screen changed viewpoints and showed her face. "Now what?"

A gunshot sounded through her mic. "I guess he was the one who was naive. Should I go back and get a sample of his blood?"

"Julie—you are a piece of work. I have a three-man team waiting to escort you out of the building. Leave your car and exit through the main entrance."

"That's better anyway. I don't think the receptionist would validate my parking."

Everyone around the table looked at Val. She sat down as if surprised to be standing. "I'm afraid we underestimated our opponent."

"Demitri, what's your assessment?"

"They respond quickly to exposure threats—executing allies by draining their blood shows sophistication. In that brief meeting, they identified us by name. We're up against a formidable organization. Blackwood knew this. He chose suicide over facing vampire assassins." Demitri put his hand to his chin and hesitated, "We just took the *All or Nothing* bat and hit a hornet's nest. If we hope to survive—we run and hide."

"Do you think they actually have nuclear capability, or was that some sort of bluff?" Val asked.

"To tell you the truth, there are so many shipping container nukes around the world, I'm not sure why nations bother to put warheads on missiles any longer. We can assume if they are desperate enough to tell us their capabilities and how they plan to respond to threats—they will not hesitate to go nuclear."

Val considered the screen. The camera showed Julie was heading down a flight of stairs, her breathing little affected by the fast pace. "Julie, we cannot seem to get governments interested in apprehending those who traffic in children, but I suspect we can get their help to clean up some misplaced nukes. Are you with me?"

"Hooah," Julie replied.

"Just remember, I was the one dissenting vote. I wanted to keep the quantum computer. Because of what we're up against, and what we need to do, we sure could use it now," Marco said.

"You don't seem to trust me very much," Val said with a sly smile. "My new friend Olin Ou agreed to let us use it anytime we like."

"Well played," Marco said. "But what about getting out of here? Their intelligence is equal to ours—maybe better. If we can track down their people, they can find us."

"Marco, you've come a long way and you are right. I'll leave it up to you and Demitri to determine how we scatter into the wind and disappear, but I need to make sure Julie is out of harm's way first. So please—shut up."

All eyes were on Julie's video stream as she continued down the empty stairway. The pace of her breathing had picked up by the time she stopped descending the stairs. She faced a solid door and whispered to herself, "I do this every day." The door opened and she walked into a large lobby area with two men staring right at her.

"They're ours!" Demitri confirmed.

"Hey, Val, thanks for the exciting look into corporate America, but I'd rather be wearing fatigues marching through a jungle with my carbine at low ready."

One man took up a position in front of her and bypassed the large revolving door, choosing one of the break-away doors off to the side instead. A black Cadillac Escalade waited for them. She got in and put her camera to the selfie view. Julie beamed, "I love Cadillacs! Can I keep it?"

Val looked relieved and teased, "Julie, here I thought you liked the jungle and combat boots. For a car like that, I'd have to station you in a city, and you'd need to get used to skyscrapers and heels." She hesitated, then added softly, "I'm glad you're safe. Goodbye for now. I'm afraid I'll be out of touch for a while."

Julie tried to say something, but no words came out. She forced her expression into a polite smile and said, "Out."

Chapter 27

THE SCREENS WENT DARK and grave faces matched the silence.

"Demitri is right. *If we hope to survive—we run and hide.* To succeed, we will need to live long enough to fight another day," Val said as she leaned back in her chair, obviously distressed. "For now, we go our separate ways and meditate on all we've learned. I want to make certain the risk we are taking eventually takes down Kozhaev's organization and everyone associated with it. If we don't live, that's one thing, but if the data gets destroyed, they will get away with murder. Gentlemen, make duplicates of the tape-drive data and distribute a copy to everybody leaving this boat tonight."

"What about the *Elysium Prime*? Is it safe for you on board?" Julian asked.

"They targeted Pavel's jet solely because of his presence. We'll split up and maintain a low profile." She looked around the room and smiled. "None of us will be on board and we all have experience disappearing. But you don't." She turned to Demitri and asked, "Do you have any recommendations for Julian?"

Demitri appeared tentative as he leaned in, "They don't know that we borrowed someone from the outside for this operation. Julian, it would be a good idea to be discreet, but you don't need to go dark. Maybe move away from your regular haunts—at least for a while."

"I've been needing to move forward. If Mitch hasn't misplaced my boat, I think I can find a warmer place to spend the winter," Julian said.

Demitri placed a hand on Julian's shoulder, then walked out of the room. Marco and Justin said nothing and headed for the galley, leaving Julian and Val alone.

Val met his eyes in silent understanding. "I'm exhausted," Val confessed.

"Me too," Julian said.

"Demitri is not one to delay. He will expect you in The Ballast to get your duplicate and he'll tell you how you must leave the yacht. Our window for getting out of here unnoticed is closing and a quick escape is essential for our success. First, I've got to get the crew off the *Elysium Prime*, but I'll see you in a few minutes."

"Here is your flash drive." Demitri handed Julian the small storage device. "Protect it with your life," he added. "Also, you've got to make it back to your marina on your own. Take this." Demitri placed a compact pistol into Julian's other hand.

"What's this for?"

"Come on, Julian. I know the State confiscated your Glock. Consider it a replacement, one that will ensure you get back to your boat. It's getting dark already and cities are deceitful."

"You know this could get me into a lot of trouble if the authorities catch me."

"Or it could save your life. But it's your choice."

Julian pocketed the drive, a hint of a smirk playing on his lips. He cautiously examined the pistol, its cold heft a comfort in his hand. In a methodical, almost ritualistic manner, he ejected the magazine, loaded with hollow-point 9mm ammunition, and racked the slide back to its locked position.

"A Walther PPS," he murmured with a nod of approval. "I like it. Thanks." There was a flash of satisfaction in his eyes.

As he reinserted the magazine into the gun, his thoughts briefly wandered. *What have I gotten into?* He released the slide lock with a press of his thumb. The abrupt click as he chambered a round snapped him back to the moment. He clipped the inside waistband holster to his belt, just behind his right hip, and carefully secured the weapon. Julian's eyes swept the room, his thoughts racing ahead to future scenarios. The cool contour of the hidden pistol pressing against his side served as a reminder of the unyielding path he had chosen. Julian pulled his shirt over the pistol's grip to conceal his new weapon.

Demitri checked the security monitor. Chuckling, he said, "Justin just morphed seamlessly into a dock boy. He tied up a small yacht, and is holding the owner's poodle as they walk down the pier. Marco is a little further down, hanging out, smoking a cigarette."

He turned his attention towards Julian. "You almost forgot your mug. My gift to you." The tall Russian reached across the desk, grabbed a mug with Cyrillic lettering and handed it to him with a big smile. He gave him a friendly hug and said, "We will meet again, my friend. You must go. Cedric has the launch waiting for you off the port side. I've found a place to put you ashore, that won't draw attention, or create a connection to your marina, but you'll have to walk the rest of the way." He smiled, said, *"Poka,"* then lowered his eyes and turned away.

After leaving Demitri, he headed directly to the port side landing to find Cedric waiting in the launch. But what caught his attention was the mistress of the *Elysium Prime* standing in a shadow off to one side. Julian walked up to her and said, "I've got a really nice sailboat. Do you need a lift?"

Val brought her hand to her chest, inhaling deeply, her smile blossoming with a mix of wistfulness and joy. "Oh, Julian, you are getting to know me! I can resist anything... except temptation!" She laughed in a carefree way, wrapped her arms around herself and looked upwards with a smile on her face. "I won't forget the stars.

"But now, I must go alone. Captain Ted, on one of Olin Ou's sailboats, the *GalaxSea II*, is going to take me on as crew for a race tomorrow. I will disappear in Victoria." Val reached her arms around Julian and allowed the embrace to linger. She released him, tilted her face upward, gave him a quick kiss on the lips and then raced off without a word.

Julian standing next to Cedric in the elegant launch gazed towards the city. The electric powered motor boat skimmed quietly over Elliot Bay's calm waters. Seattle looked tranquil, but distant sirens and the sporadic flash of red and blue lights confirmed Demitri's comment about *deceit*. Surveillance drones dotted the sky over the streets. Their watchful presence, a reminder of what had become the new normal.

Cedric kept a wide berth from shore as they skirted Discovery Park. The water treatment facility was lit up like a prison camp, creating a clear demarcation between civilization and occupied territory where even the police wouldn't dare enter. Weak campfires gave evidence of people living amidst the wooded public space. A bonfire along the beach drew Julian's eyes, the music blaring from competing sound systems mingled into an amorphous din. Cedric steered a course even farther from shore. Someone yelled out in a loud enraged voice, followed by a couple gunshots. Julian instinctively ducked and Cedric pushed the throttles.

The north shore wasn't any better, but as they turned into the Salmon Bay Waterway everything was quiet and Cedric surprised him when he made a sharp left turn and slowed into the beachfront of a small mansion.

"You'll have to get your feet wet. One of Val's friends owns this. The access code is very original. I hope you can remember it—two-zero-two-zero. That will get you through the gate into the private garden. Then just go up to the road. Good luck from there." He shook Julian's hand.

"Thank you, Cedric. Thanks for the advice."

"What advice?"

"You told me Val doesn't bite. That knowledge helped me more than you can imagine."

"Oh, yes. I said, *she doesn't bite strangers*. Now you're one of us, so watch out!"

"It doesn't look like I'll ever see her again, so I'm not worried."

Cedric smiled and laughed, "We'll see."

By the time Julian punched the access code into the gate at the marina, his feet were sore and he was dead tired. He walked past the empty slip which had been graced by *Sapphire*, Mitch's beautiful Concordia yawl. Two boats away, the *Horizon's Edge* looked happy to greet him. A light even shown from below decks. She seemed to sit just a little lower in the water than he remembered. It all made sense after he got on board.

"Don't freak out. I'm not gone yet."

Julian did not freak out. Seeing the open hatch and hearing Mitch's rumbling voice coming out of the companionway, came as a relief. "Did you have a pleasant cruise? Aren't the San Juan Islands amazing?" He walked down the companionway into the salon and sat on the settee across from Mitch.

Mitch handed him a beer and said, "Indeed they are. I hear you had a successful cruise too—at least until you pissed off the bad guys."

"You got that right," Julian said.

"Val told me you are one of us. Of course, I knew you despised the tyrannical overreach of the government, but talk is cheap. She assures me you are a trusted member of the rebellion. Can I expect to see a Gadsden flag flying from your backstay?"

"I've learned a lot in the last couple days. For instance, I know that is a trick question. It is very unwise for a rebel to announce that he or she intends to take on an entrenched establishment. So, no, I will not be advertising my resistance." Julian folded his arms and gave his head a conclusive nod in a gesture of triumph.

"Well played! What are your plans now?"

"They told me to lie low for a while. I was thinking I'd sail my way down south. It's something I've always dreamed of."

"What about Emily and Asher?"

Julian hesitated before answering. "A couple of days ago, I was unwilling to leave them. Now, I think it might be the best thing. Emily told me she wanted to bring Asher and spend Christmas vacation on the boat. I'm going to hold her to that, no matter where the *Horizon's Edge* is floating. It will be better for us to be away from here—fewer distractions. Besides, she'd never turn down an all expense paid trip to paradise."

"Sounds like a wonderful idea. And it fits right into what I've schemed up. I'm sure you noticed *Sapphire* isn't in her slip."

"Where is she?"

"I had her hauled out today. She is getting new bottom paint. I needed to get that done before I sailed south myself. The only problem is the yard is two weeks out. Also, you will not be surprised to find that I must lie low myself. So, I took some liberties figuring you'd agree to take me on as crew."

"What are you talking about?" Julian asked.

"Look, I need to sail away too. You need someone with blue water experience to help you sail to winter cruising grounds. It is the perfect arrangement. When we get your boat down to the edge of freedom, we'll fly back up and sail *Sapphire* down together. Win-win."

Julian took a moment to think about Mitch's offer. "That actually sounds like a brilliant plan. I'm in."

Mitch rose to his feet, walked over to Julian and extended his hand.

Julian stood and started to extend his hand, then pulled it back suddenly. "Wait just one minute. I have one condition and it is non-negotiable."

"Okay, what?"

"Under no circumstances will you throw me off the boat."

"Deal!" and the two shook hands. "I hope you don't mind. I've taken some liberties with your boat. I topped off the fuel and fresh water tanks. Pumped the holding tank, and restocked the fridge and resupplied your pantry."

"Well, thanks? I get the tanks, but you resupplied the pantry? That seems a little over the top."

"Not really. I was expecting you to agree to my plan. We've got enough food onboard to last the two of us a month."

"A month?"

"Yeah, we need to leave soon and I didn't want any excuses."

"How soon?"

"Tonight. Right after Emily and Asher come and say goodbye."

Julian sat down. "Are you kidnapping me again?"

Mitch gave a cautious smile and said, "Maybe you should think of it as pressed into service."

"I don't know how you got all this together so fast. I won't even ask about the permits to escape state and federal waters, but how did you arrange for my daughter and grandson to come for a visit? I haven't seen them in two months and... it's a school night!"

"What can I say? My friends tell me I'm very persuasive."

The sound of footsteps on the topsides interrupted Julian's response. He moved to the foot of the companionway steps and beamed at Asher. The boy looked excited to see his poppa. He grabbed the companionway hatch, swung and hung from his arms knowing his grandfather would grab him and lower him into the salon.

"Asher, you've grown since I saw you last. You're getting stronger too!"

Emily followed Asher, but used the stairs. "Hi, Dad."

"Hi, Honey. It's wonderful to see you. Thanks for coming."

"This is my friend, Mitch."

"I know. We've met."

"When?"

"Today. Didn't you know? He tracked down Jonathan." She glanced over to Mitch and smiled.

She hugged her dad and said, "I didn't know your new friend was a PI until he came over and explained that you had hired him to help me. Thank you for doing that. Jonathan wouldn't answer my calls and neither would his mom. I didn't know what to do. But Mitch did. He had a pizza delivered to his mom's house and paid the delivery guy to give him a message." She shot Mitch a quizzical glance and continued. "He won't tell me what the message said, but Jonathan called me right away. We talked for about an hour. Mitch played soccer with Asher the whole time. Dad, you were right about Jonathan. He's a jerk!"

Julian marveled how he could both feel bad for his daughter and elated at the same time. He simply said, "I'm sorry, Emily. Is there anything I can do to help you right now?"

"Yes, take us away from here!"

"Really?"

"No." She gave a playful hand slap into his shoulder. "I'm an adult and have a life. I have work and Asher has school. Tomorrow!" She looked over to Asher as he played tic-tac-toe with Mitch. "Dad, you've already been a big help.

"But that's enough about me. Mitch told me about what happened to you!"

"He did? What did he tell you?"

"Congratulations, Dad! I'm so happy for you. I'm glad you're moving on. They never really appreciated your skills at the university. It's great that you've decided to take on a new job and it sounds like a perfect fit. Imagine, you can work from anywhere in the world." She wrinkled her nose. "I know mom would have been so proud of you. And working for a non-profit is commendable. You'll be helping children! Mom would have loved that part."

In that moment, Julian realized the information Emily had reported about his new life could only have come from Mitch. It was time to play along and enjoy the enthusiasm of his daughter. "Yeah. You know, you were right too. I needed to make progress and move on with my life. Having a new direction feels great. Did Mitch tell you he's the one who helped me get the new job?"

"No. But it doesn't surprise me."

"Did he tell you we are sailing south for the winter?"

"Of course, that's why we're here. To wish you a bon voyage. But I don't see why you have to leave tonight... in the dark."

Mitch got up from the table. "The weather is optimal."

Julian, adding his own improvisation, said, "And you know me. The tide is going out. All mariners know to leave on the ebb tide." He looked at the marine clock mounted in the nav station, then added, "In fact, we need to set sail pretty soon."

Mitch nodded in agreement.

"I'm glad you'll have good weather. It makes it easier to say goodbye. We have to get going anyway. I have to get Asher to bed."

Julian suddenly looked concerned, "Emily, where did you park? It isn't safe to drive around at night."

"No worries, Dad. Mitch arranged a ride for us."

"He did?"

Mitch beamed. "How do you like it?"

"Well, I feel safe. But guilty too. I'm sure the fuel used in that beast is ruining the world."

"It's so cool. The biggest, blackest car I've ever seen. Like in the movies! Willy is our driver and Julie is our bodyguard," Asher said excitedly.

Mitch said, "Julie is capable, but her husband, Willy, is quite the character. I've got a story about him that I'll share on our southbound journey. They're helping us out tonight with the limo service for your family before their dinner reservation." He checked his watch. "Which is in an hour."

"I told them we wouldn't be long," Emily said. "Asher, give your poppa a hug goodbye." A look of disgust fell over her face. "They probably didn't even turn off the engine."

Emily shook hands with Mitch. "Thank you so much for all you've done for us. I wish we had more time to get to know you. Asher couldn't stop talking about how you made the soccer ball spin into the goal." She gave her dad a hug and kissed him on the cheek before they left. "I love you."

When they were gone, he punched Mitch a little too hard on the shoulder and said, "I'm glad you're so persuasive, but I'm thinking there might come a time when I'll resent it."

"My grandmother used to say, 'Don't borrow worry.' I think that's wise advice, don't you?"

"Great advice," Julian replied and sat down with a grin on his face. "I'm going to help you get out of the marina and then I'm going straight to bed. If you wake me for anything, other than a genuine emergency, you'll be polishing all the stainless steel on this ship."

Mitch straightened and squared his shoulders. He gave a crisp salute. "Aye aye, Captain."

Epilogue

ASHER PLAYED FREELY ON the beach with two slightly older boys. His near-white blond hair contrasted with a deep tan. They had shifted from digging in the wet sand to engaging in a spirited game of tug-of-war with a scrap of rope. Laughter filled the air as the animated rope fiercely pulled them, held tension, and then wriggled like a serpent. With each effort the boys put in, the *snake* renewed its vigor, intensifying their laughter until the playful antics stopped and the rope went limp. The boys dropped to the sand, panting, and their faces lit up with deep satisfaction.

If their mothers were present to witness this epic battle of youthful exuberance, they wisely remained in the shade, allowing the boys to revel in their carefree play without guidance or interference. This was the side of Asher's new life that his grandfather cherished—a series of spontaneous moments, some marked by frustration, others by challenges, but most filled with pure joy.

Months had passed since Emily and Asher joined Julian aboard *Horizon's Edge*. A Christmas vacation that became permanent and blossomed into so much more. The stifling, overly-controlled life they had all known in Seattle felt like a distant dream. They were thriving in a *new normal*, one where the roots of freedom were taking hold, nurturing Asher's growth into the man he would eventually become.

As the boys picked up their rope and sought refuge under the shade of the coconut trees, Julian's phone rang. Since only Emily and Mitch had his new number, he didn't bother checking the caller ID. "Hola," he greeted.

"It's wonderful to hear your voice. We should have had more time together. Perhaps someday soon."

Julian felt a rush of emotion that momentarily made his heart race. But, as the feeling passed, a wide smile spread across his face. He sat down, steadying himself against a rock the size of a bench. "You're alive!"

"Don't act so surprised. Why would you ever believe news reports?"

"At first, I didn't. But Mitch did some digging, and eventually we were convinced they had taken you out."

"Well, the reports were... exaggerated. It turns out, if someone really wants to disappear and that someone has a friend with a quantum computer, it's rather easy to *die*."

"Val, where are you?" Julian asked.

"No, no. Our old friend, Val—she is truly dead. There is truth in the reports," she sighed audibly. "I needed to call you to admit I was wrong. It turns out my genes had no power to keep me from finding God after all. I'm still deeply flawed, but I've found peace. As you are aware, He works in mysterious ways. Blood! That's it Julian. That's it.... the blood of Jesus. Such irony is so wonderful—truly indescribable!"

He was both elated and confused, leaving him feeling bewildered, yet grounded with the sandy rock pressing into his bones. He found comfort in the absolutes of universal forces. Smiling, he asked, "Well, sister, what do I call you now?"

"You can call me Lilia. I must go now, but I wanted you to see this picture. When we next meet, tell me what you saw in the photo?"

He cupped his hand to shade the screen and peered at the image on his phone. Her hair was pulled back, neatly concealed by a headscarf. She wore a peasant blouse with a loosely tied knot forming a casual collar. Her eyes, vibrant with life, twinkled with intensity. They amplified the smile lines that graced her face, each one telling its own story. There was confidence in her gaze, showing a wisdom that only comes with age. In her right hand, she held a hatchet, her other leaned playfully against a wood round, made for chopping. Beside her stood a freshly split stack of kindling, and he could see a bushel basket loaded with cucumbers to her other side. But at the center of the image, suspended from a braided fiber necklace, hung a cross crafted from horseshoe nails bound by a wire.

Before he could utter a word, the call abruptly ended, and the image disappeared. Julian slid the phone into his pocket with a warm smile on his face. As he observed Asher playing with his friends under the trees, a profound sense of contentment washed over him. She was alive.

"Hey, Julian, look what the cat dragged in."

He wiped away an unexpected tear as he turned towards Mitch's low rumbling voice.

Since finding the protected anchorage, the retired naval officer had been an excellent influence on Julian. Their boats, *Sapphire* and *Horizon's Edge*, tugged at their moorings. Each morning, Mitch and Julian would start with a quick swim to shore, followed by a beachside workout led by Mitch. By the time Emily and Asher arrived in the dinghy, the men were enjoying coffee at the only open restaurant. The plastic yard chairs and rickety table embedded in the sand on the edge of the beach perfectly suited their morning ritual. Julian had become even more physically fit with the daily exercise and the rigors of living on a boat, but he could not keep up with Mitch's ability to handle, with ease, the sun and the heat of the day. Both men seemed to thrive in this new environment as if they were preparing for a unique, yet unknown destiny. Their routine had grown to satisfy everyone. After coffee, while Mitch continued his workouts with runs on the dirt roads or kayaking offshore, Julian kept an eye on Asher as Emily helped her new boyfriend prepare the restaurant's lunch menu. But today was different—Mitch returned early, bringing another shocking surprise.

As tall and strong as Mitch was, Demitri still towered over the much older man and made him look average. When the Russian cybersecurity expert dropped his large backpack and turned on his smile, Julian had no choice but to steel himself against the bearhug he knew was coming.

Demitri released Julian and said, "I come bearing gifts and glad tidings. I see Asher, but where is Emily?" His attitude stayed playful, but an undercurrent of urgency in his words added a more serious dimension.

Julian checked the time on his Islander dive watch. "She's in town buying fresh seafood for Ricardo's restaurant." He made a fist and used his thumb to point behind him to the small shack poised at the convergence of jungle and the sandy beach.

"I know I just got here, and I hate to push, but she needs to hear what I have to say. Can we go get her? I need to talk to everybody—on your boat."

"Asher," Julian yelled. "Take your friends and go get your mom. Tell her she has to come back here right away. It cannot wait!"

The boys ran off without hesitation, chasing and laughing as they sprinted in zig zags, tagging each other just for fun.

Mitch chuckled, "Demitri, you're looking pretty good for a dead man, but you still look wiped. As for me, I'm starting to dry up here, and Julian? He can't even handle a bit of sun. It'll take at least fifteen minutes for Emily to get back here. What do you say I buy a round of beers?" Mitch turned and walked across the sand to his usual seat under the awning. Calling out, *"Tres cervezas por favor."*

"If you're here, you must be in contact with Val," Julian said.

"What are you talking about?" Mitch asked.

"I just talked to Val on the phone. She sent me a picture."

Demitri glared at Julian. "Val is dead." He reached a long arm across to Mitch and gripped his shoulder tightly. "We will not speak of the dead here. It does no honor to her. When we are back on the *Horizon's Edge*, I will offer a toast to our fallen comrade. Until then," he raised his bottle of beer and said, "I salute—we the living."

Julian got the feeling that Demitri's *toast to the living* was about more than just a nudge not to talk about the dead. One thing he was sure of—Demitri turning up right after Val's call wasn't a coincidence.

"I fought with your poppa in the war. He is a hero. And me? They commanded me to keep him alive."

Asher's eyes opened wide, and he moved in closer to the giant of a man who wove a tall tale that sparked his imagination.

Keeping his eyes on the boy, Demitri reached across the cockpit, grabbed the backpack and placed it between his knees like Santa Claus about to hand out presents. "So, I am giving you a very special gift." He hesitated. "Wait a minute. How old are you?"

"Almost eight," Asher answered.

He whispered, "Well, that's how old I was when I got mine, but what about your mom? Should I ask her if it's okay? Maybe she will want me to wait a year or two."

Asher looked over to Julian and seemed to gain a measure of confidence. "It will be okay. She always tells me I need to act my age," he said, beaming with a hopeful smile. "My birthday is in a week."

"Do you think you're ready though? What I am about to give you will teach you how to fight. You'll learn how to destroy the evil king and free the people. It's important training, but it's not for everybody." Demitri opened the top of his backpack and carefully retrieved an unlikely package, neatly wrapped with tidy edges. The straw-colored string encircled each edge until it finally ended in a bow. He handed the present to the excited boy. "Open it!"

Julian chuckled while Asher eagerly tore into the package, casting furtive glances toward the companionway as if dreading his mother's return. But when he unveiled the wooden box, with brown and tan squares, he showed it for all to see, confident his claim to the present had been secured.

"Do you know what it is?" Demitri asked.

"It's a chessboard."

"You're not wrong. But it is more, a battlefield of brains. If you think you are ready for the game of kings, open it up." With both hands Demitri mimicked the motion of opening up the hinged case.

The grin on Asher's face couldn't have been wider as he worked the clasp, unveiled the contents and drew out a hand carved knight. "Wow! I've always wanted a chess set. Thanks!"

"You can thank me by becoming as skilled as your poppa. He will teach you all you need to know," he said with a wink.

Julian thought, *presentation is everything*. He had a chess set and had offered to teach Asher, but his grandson always chose Battleship or more often, went off on his own to play Minecraft. He felt a surge of excitement at the thought of Asher learning and mastering the game. Alongside this joy, there was a hint of wistfulness, as he considered the swift passage of time and the bittersweet nature of watching his grandson grow up in a challenging world.

Demitri pulled out a bottle and handed it to Mitch with a wink. "From Lilia. It is Vana Tallinn, Estonia's pride. It's a unique mix of rum and aromatic spices, perfect straight, on the rocks or in coffee. You'll love it."

Mitch grasped the bottle. "You do not know how weak my coffee has been lately. Thank you, fine sir, and I'll make sure to send a card to Lilia."

"Emily. Just in time. Here's some of my homeland's finest honey, a natural taste of our rich beekeeping heritage." As she moved from the companionway across the cockpit to find a seat in the shade, Demitri handed her a small glass pot the color of toasted amber with a wax seal.

"Thank you. But what's this I hear about turning Asher into a warrior? I'll have none of that!"

"It's just a chessboard, Mom. I can keep it, can't I?" Asher asked cautiously.

"Well, that seems pretty harmless," Emily agreed.

"For you, Julian, I have the most significant gift of all. But I must insist we go below—alone." Demitri wasted no time and hurried down the steps into the dim light of the salon.

"Wow! Do you have air conditioning?"

Proud that Demitri noticed his accomplishment, Julian offered a content smile. "We do, but almost never use it. Too big a drain on the electrical system. What you are enjoying is the sweet balance of shade, a very effective wind scoop and an efficient low voltage heat exchanger I dreamed up. The shade keeps the deck cooler, the wind scoop collects the air and funnels it across the solar powered seawater cooled heat exchanger and bingo... even you could survive the tropics! As long as there is a breeze, it's much cooler down here than on deck."

"It's so lush here and beautiful, but I think I'll stick to living in the northern latitudes. But when I get old like you and Mitch—who knows? Maybe one day."

"Ouch! I can take that kind of remark. I just turned sixty-one and feel twenty years younger, but you better be careful with Mitch. He's pretty sensitive about his age."

Demitri extended his arm across the back of the settee and asked, "What do you know about the aftermath of our operation's unraveling?"

"Since Mitch and I weren't as connected to Val as you were, we've been enjoying a leisurely cruise down the left coast. When we discovered this little slice of paradise, we stopped. A few months back, the media reported that *Elysium Prime* sank in a storm and said that Val and her crew, except for the cook, perished. The world mourned, but Mitch and I were skeptical. It wasn't until he checked with his sources and we learned you all returned to *Elysium Prime* some days before the catastrophic loss at sea. All, that is, except for Justin." Julian's eyes darted upwards as if looking for an answer that wasn't to be found. He strained his face, trying to match what he knew with the fresh revelations. "We saw photographs and read government reports. The only two bodies that were recovered were Marcos' and Val's. Mitch showed me the autopsy reports complete with pictures of their partially decomposed corpses." He shuddered. "The morgue photographs were definitely of Marcos and Val. We had given up hope—until just a few minutes ago, that is. I'm ecstatic to see you, and I'm thrilled that Val, I mean Lilia, is alive."

"I must admit, being a ghost has some advantages. But forgive me, I should start at the beginning. After we parted, so much happened. Remember Olin Ou?"

"Of course! The billionaire inventor of the Madras Motor. The guy who Val gave her late husband's quantum computer to. It's not something you forget."

"I guess not," Demitri shrugged. "Well, Val sailed away to Vancouver on one of his racing yachts. But before she left Seattle, she secured an escape for Marco and me. Justin decided it was time for him to make his own way in the world and refused any help, including a bug-out bag that Val offered him. He ended up hiding among Seattle's homeless community until he got cold and hunted down Megan Ward. He asked her for refuge and a job. He didn't show up for our return to the *Elysium Prime* because he's still lying low and working off-the-books for what's left of Genesis Security.

"Val gave Olin a heads up that Marco and I needed a *get out of jail free card* and he stole us away, before we drank too much that very evening. We helped him get Pavel's quantum computer up and running. As you know, other than the quantum processor, the two major aspects of a quantum computer are power and cooling. But Olin added another brilliant component—obscurity. Before Olin even knew about Val and her extraordinary gift, he had built a vault under a river. It's amazing. Someday, I hope you can visit. The underwater site solved many problems, including consistent, free hydroelectricity and endless cooling potential. The bonus of being hidden from inquisitive eyes served us well. I cannot tell you where it is, but I can say it is so remote, he never asked for permission or bothered to get a construction permit. We lived there for a couple months and never saw a soul, even on the security cameras during hunting season."

"I don't get it. I'm guessing it was all a ruse going back on the *Elysium Prime,* but why? That was an incredible yacht. What a waste!" Julian said.

"Really? Is that what you're worried about? Anyway, it is now an artificial reef. You can visit with scuba gear if you like."

"Oh, good. Let's plan a dive trip," Julian joked.

"I've got a better idea, but first you need to understand that Olin is always six moves ahead. He had been working on developing his own AI, and he had come a very long way without a quantum computer. But for his next advancement, he needed one, so he did that thing..." Demitri screwed up his face and looked around the salon as if searching for something he lost. "You know. It was an American movie about baseball? About building it..."

"*Field of Dreams*!?"

"Yes, that's it. *Build it, and it will show up.*"

"You mean, *Build it, and they will come,*" Julian corrected.

"Of course. Anyway, even though Olin could afford it, he didn't want to draw any attention to himself by commissioning his own quantum processor. He developed the infrastructure and built the vault. Then, like the movie, Val shows up with a quantum processor for his *Field of Dreams*.

"Marco and I moved in and got to work with Olin's team and it wasn't long before we realized Ava could arrange an accident to fake our deaths. The result would allow us to start fresh and stop looking over our shoulders."

"Wait. Who is Ava?" Julian asked.

"Oh, sorry. Ava is Olin's AI. She is quite amazing and as near to sentient as I have ever imagined, with hacking skills you can only dream of. The accident was child's play for her. Even getting the right bodies from the morgue and altering the biometrics and dental records to match us took her only seconds. The deeper someone looked into the deaths, the more convinced they would become that we all died that fateful day.

"There was only one person on the *Elysium Prime* when she hit a rock and went down in the storm. The man who survived told the coast guard he was the cook when they picked him up by helicopter. In reality, he was a stuntman Val had worked with in film years ago. He got his chance to be the star of this drama as he recounted his own perils and the tragic death of Val and the rest of the crew."

"Amazing! So, why now? What are you doing here?" Julian asked.

"We need you. The nukes. They're all dismantled. Turns out there were four, not three. But there is not a country in the world who wants a containerized nuclear device sitting on their soil. Once we pointed them out, they took the threats seriously and disabled the damn things."

"How in the world did you find them?"

"Ava. She has been amazing. She even made it appear that the military and law enforcement agencies did the hard work of discovery. At that point, Val gave us the green light to track down every one of Kozhaev's clients." Demitri clapped his hands together. "Now, we are going to take the bastards out."

"Why do you need me? It sounds like this Ava AI can do anything I can do and far faster. Plus, I've been working on my copy of the *All or Nothing* list, and I found no way through the encryption. I began to wonder if those few names we hacked were left out as low fruit, to lure us in. Probably to use as a sacrifice to attract and eventually hunt down anybody out to get them. In all this time alone with the list, I only uncovered two more names. The hardware and software might be vintage 1980, but the encryption is beyond anything I can help with."

"Ava has already taken care of that. She finished deciphering what was on the tape drive long before the *Elysium Prime* went down. Now, with the nukes secure, we developed a plan to take down Kozhaev and everyone associated with him. We also found we were dealing with thousands of individuals. All of them are connected to the global elite, and many are highly placed in governments. I have seen the list. The majority are protected by the strength of their nation's secret service, loyal law enforcement, or military. The rest have varying degrees of access to quantities of guns, money and lawyers.

"The scope of this operation makes taking out four nukes look like a simple matter. That's why we have taken so long to take action. We needed to be certain that the execution of our plan would work.

"I think you can appreciate that our tactics must be perfectly coordinated and occur within hours—not days. The sophistication involved is monumental, but Ava is a grandmaster with strategic planning, and we are primed to release our attack in a little over a week. Mitch is not involved in any of this, but I know he supports our cause. Plus, I'm sure he will stay here and see that your family is cared for while you are gone."

"I know I'm repeating myself, but why do you need me? This feels a lot like when I was on *Elysium Prime* trying to figure out why I had been kidnapped," Julian said.

"Sure, but now you are one of us, committed to seeing it through, and if I recall... even to death. Right now, what we need most is loyalty. There is still much to do in preparation, and we are recruiting people we know we can count on. People we can trust with our lives."

"Thanks for the reminder," Julian said with sarcasm. "Where are we going? No, wait. Don't answer. Judging from Val's picture, it looks like she is living the life of a survivalist? My first guess was that she went back to Donbas to her roots, but from your gifts, I'm thinking maybe Estonia. They have top-notch internet and connectivity to everywhere in the world. As nation-states go, they look the other way and stay out of people's business. It would be the perfect place for a couple of Russians to hang out and start new lives."

Demitri sat up and gave Julian a quiet applause. "Well done. You have just completed Spy 101. Yes, that is where we are going. Most of the programmers and logistic experts we have on board are remote, but your cell connection here just won't cut it. Plus, there is a personal matter that is of the highest importance." His smile flashed white in the low light before he said, "But I must first deal with our cause of liberty and justice for all.

"Val told you our revolution is not an armed uprising. To us, guns are only for self defense. Since lies oppress people, we expose the truth. We didn't begin our revolution with any knowledge regarding the depth of human trafficking and how deeply it is woven into the globalist and transhuman agenda. Consider us naive, but those days have passed, and our eyes are wide open. Now, we understand if we take down Kozhaev and his associates, we are instantly advancing our core cause of fostering liberty."

"I appreciate your vision, but how in the world can you hope to expose these villains? I have no reason to doubt they are among the most powerful individuals, but knowing who they are is not the same as taking them down."

"You're right. It is messy and won't be easy. Some tactics will work, and some will not. Unfortunately, we cannot hope to win the war, but we can reveal extensive corruption and break up Kozhaev's system." Demitri shifted in his seat and stretched out his legs. "The corporate sponsored media outlets always read from the same script. The talking heads are so used to not thinking, it will take them a couple of hours before they realize they didn't get their script through the normal channels—from the intelligentsia. That is more than enough time for citizen journalists to run with the truth. At that point, the media will distract the viewers with some sensational twaddle about threats of foreign wars or some Hollywood scandals. The more tyrannical nations will simply turn off the internet completely. Law enforcement, including military police, will be forced to do Ava's bidding—human trafficking is still a crime. We have mountains of irrefutable evidence of a myriad of illegal activities, including racketeering, smuggling, money laundering, drug trafficking, extortion and bribery. As you know, many of Kozhaev's clients are complicit in the kidnapping, torture and death of children.

"Even though the criminality is terrifying, Ava predicts only about twenty percent of these bastards are susceptible to arrest. The rest are virtually above the law, so it would be a waste of time to subject them to the legal system of their respective countries. All we can hope for is to uncover Kozhaev's methods, revealing names and putting the truth out for the public to see. The key is to deliver all this information at one time. We cannot give them time to shut us down, redact the evidence or spin this story. We saw how quickly they moved in to kill Kozhaev's clients after we identified them. There is no question they have deep and impressive resources, and we must adapt. Just like with our acquisition of the data on the tape drive, this is another *All or Nothing* proposal. We hope to deliver all we've got, before they can react." Demitri shifted his head to the side and grinned like a naughty child who enjoyed being bad. "We call it

Operation Truth Bomb. As soon as our payload is delivered, we shut it down, cut all ties and go silent.

"When the dust settles, every criminal will be exposed. We will have to be content to sit back and see if society cares more for their children or their kings." He inhaled slowly and looked concerned. "Now, Julian, do you have any questions, or can I get on with my personal request?"

"Oh, I have a million questions. But I'm learning to trust the methods of my new fraternity. You *give-me-liberty-or-give-me-death* Russians are a patient lot, so I will allow you to answer as we journey on. Personal? This is a first for you and me."

Demitri stood up and almost hit his head on the ceiling. "I respect you, and I know from your dossier that you are a believer. I'm getting married and would like you to officiate the wedding."

Julian rose to his feet, extending his hand in a gesture of solemn commitment. "I'm honored, Demitri. Absolutely."

"I can't wait for you to meet her! Olga is stunning, truly the most beautiful woman in the world. And guess what? It was my grandmother who played matchmaker! Olga's family owns a bakery, where she works." He pushed his phone towards Julian with a big smile.

Julian imagined Demitri's fiancé would be a simple-looking, wholesome girl from a backward village. When he saw the engagement picture, he exclaimed, "She is beautiful! What is she, six feet tall? My goodness, she could be a supermodel. What a handsome couple you two make. Congratulations."

Demitri scrolled through the pictures and showed him another. "This is a popular women's magazine, and it featured Olga on the cover," he said, laughing. "That was when she was a supermodel! Around the same time I gave up being a spy, she gave up her modeling career. Since then, we dated on and off. However, when it was reported that I had died at sea, she became distraught and grieved. Two days later, I showed up very much alive, with a new identity. After she nearly killed me, I asked her to marry me."

The two men sat in silence for a long moment until Demitri said, "I hope our kids get her looks and my brawn."

"I'm sure they will." Julian placed a hand on Demitri's shoulder. "I hope you are as happy together as Faith and I were."

He said, "Thank you," then stood in awkward silence.

"Demitri, what else do I need to know about *Operation Truth Bomb*?"

"Getting used to working with a super smart AI will be a whole new experience for you. Also, Val has changed—not just her name. She's still the complex person she always was, but now she's focused on improving herself. It's been amazing to witness. Don't get me wrong, she's determined as ever, yet now there's a sense of humility. While she's maintained her strong-willed nature, she's become more reflective.

"In truth, we've all changed. We've experienced a miracle. And Val? Well, you've talked to her..."

Julian didn't wait to see which of the likely emotions were about to erupt from Demitri's contorting face and asked, "What miracle?"

"Carmen Lucia Sánchez is alive."

"The little girl who they smuggled out of the US? How?"

"It seems our concern for her did more than just direct us to Kozhaev's child smuggling operation. After we lost track of the private jet over Algeria, Val prayed. No one knew; after all, she was committed to her agnostic beliefs—troubled only by evil, never by God." Demitri chuckled softly, a gleam of understanding in his eyes.

"It wasn't until Olin's smart AI inquired if we might be interested in Carmen's whereabouts that we understood the change. Why Val had died and Lilia had been born. In her testimony to our tiny congregation in Estonia, she explained she fell onto her knees and prayed—not to God, but against Satan. In time, a peace overwhelmed her and she accepted that the absence of evil is the very presence of God.

"Adding to the wonder, we found little Carmen had been reunited with her family in Honduras. When the plane landed to refuel, she broke free of her captors and ran right into the arms of an Africa Inland Mission pilot who saved her.

"Now, the old Val is very hard to find. As for Lilia, well, you'll see." With a smirk forming on Demitri's lips, he said, "It seems she's genuinely thrilled about you joining us. Marco thought he saw a spark between you two back on the *Elysium Prime,* but I told him he was crazy. She never dated after they killed Pavel even though she had plenty of opportunity, so I told Marco he saw nothing. But now, I wonder. Is there anything I should know about the two of you?"

"Not a thing," Julian said a little too quickly.

"Okay. Well, I got a weird vibe when I told her I was going to get you, and then I got it again when I saw you on the beach. It's a spy thing, and my hunches are usually correct."

"Is that what you want to talk about?" Julian asked.

"Just wondering if I missed something."

"I'm just here for the revolution. When do we leave?"

The sound of a plane roared overhead and dissipated slowly.

"Julian, are you sure you're not a spy? Your timing is impeccable. Get your things and say goodbye. That is the float plane that has come to retrieve us." Demitri was almost up the steps of the companionway when he stopped and bent himself in half to look back at Julian. "Don't worry. Mitch will probably have Asher ready to give you a good chess game when you get back.

"I'm going topside to tell Emily what's up. Get your gear together. We'll be traveling light. Bring a shaving kit, traveling clothes and a jacket. Leave all your tech here—ours is better."

His mind buzzed with excitement. Collaborating with this dedicated group, united in their passion for liberty, had brought a newfound satisfaction and purpose to Julian's life. He accepted that the tragedy of Faith's death was just as much of his life's story as were the joyful memories of all the years they had together. He still missed her terribly, however, the thought of crafting a brighter future for their legacy—Emily, Asher and their future grandchildren—seemed to have magical qualities. Joyfulness lived on.

Perhaps he was learning to be a spy after all. Even though she had not yet said anything, he knew Emily was expecting a baby. His Spanish was not good, but he heard the giggles and whispers of her and Ricardo talking about their future together. She spent more time getting ready in the morning and refrained from drinking alcohol. Anyone who paid attention would notice that she had stopped wearing bikinis and chose shorts with loose fitting tops. He knew she tried to cover the ever-increasing bulge of her tummy, but the tropics is a hard place to cover up such things and the limited privacy of a sailboat is not conducive to secrets.

Julian emerged from the companionway, his satchel full with belongings. Emily approached, her eyes shining. She embraced him tightly. "Dad, there's something I need to tell you before you leave."

"Me too. I love you," Julian said before Emily could finish.

"I love you too, Dad." She cast her eyes downward.

"I'm so happy for you and Ricardo. You know your mother was all about the babies. She dedicated her life to care for the children. I see that side of her in you. You are a wonderful mother, and I'm going to be so excited to hold my new grandbaby."

Emily wrapped her arms around her dad and squeezed tight. "Thank you, Dad. I'm so happy! Don't be gone long."

"That's up to this guy." He tossed the satchel to Demitri in the front of the small tender and stepped into the center of the boat. Mitch manned the outboard, and the motor muted any conversation until they got to the waiting floatplane.

With the engine at an idle, Mitch said, "Don't worry, my friend, I'll keep an eye on everything here. Also, I'll bring out the warrior in Asher... at least on the chessboard."

Julian situated himself in the passenger seat behind the pilot and Demitri sat where the co-pilot should have been. The plane's single engine thundered to life, its vibrations rippling across the water as it gathered speed for takeoff. He smiled, realizing God had given them all more days on earth to fulfill their purpose.

Acknowledgements

Bringing this book into your hands has been a journey paved with the remarkable dedication and support of truly incredible individuals. Elizabeth Beach meticulously edited the manuscript while Emaleigh Pierce and Sandra Mobley checked every sentence. Jim Bartlett and Kelli Grotle, as beta readers, provided critical feedback early on, and helped me refine the narrative. The technical aspects, including cybersecurity, were adeptly reviewed by Barclay Berry, Devin Courtney and Dwayne Foley.

Encouragement came from many quarters: Camano Writers, my family, friends, patients, and Archer, the distinguished K-9. Adding to this support, Yvonne Laun, Anlee Fekkes and Jim Karstetter, as advanced copy readers, extended their help and encouragement. The Christian Libertarian Institute, the Mises Institute and The Hacker News offered invaluable institutional support. Curiously, the actions of nation-states, numerous NGOs and the ambitions of megalomaniacs provided the perfect backdrop for the dystopian elements of this tale.

finlaybeach.com

Dear Reader,

Thank you for reading *The Seventh Pawn*. This is where most authors ask you to leave a positive review. But there is something you need to know before I encourage you to promote my book.

My dad, who was both a pilot and an aeronautical engineer, taught me a crucial lesson from flying: When a plane stalls and spirals, nose to the ground, disorientation worsens the situation. The key to recovery is not feelings but factual information—orientation, airspeed, altitude and rate of descent, as shown by the flight instruments. This approach allows a pilot to regain control and resume level flight. He compared this to life's crises, showing us that in turmoil, focusing on truth rather than emotions leads to stability and averts disaster.

There is plenty of evidence that humanity is in a downward spin, but that does not mean we have to panic, give up and crash. The gospel of John says, "And you will know the truth, and the truth will set you free." God also seems pretty adamant about His distribution of free will to His image bearers. We must not panic, only seek truth. There is hope woven in Scripture, through the Holy Spirit and indeed, permeating all of Creation. Realizing the significance of truth and hope illuminates the reason I'm passionate about the stories I write.

I am honored that you shared a part of your life experience by reading *The Seventh Pawn*. My goal is to write stories of consequence that entertain. While all authors share perspectives, I am challenged to provide fiction you can count on. If I do my job well, my readers will relate to the struggles and victories of my characters. If I do my job well, they'll see the worth in my stories. And if I do my job well, they'll want to pass those stories on to others.

Which leads me to that author thing—explaining how, if you loved this book, you can help others find it by taking a minute and giving me a positive review. I'm going to double down on that and ask you to share this book with friends on social media and in your in-real-life community too. If you had issues with this book, or the author, I still encourage you to leave an honest review, and tell the world exactly where I failed you. After all, feedback is vital, and that is why I'm available at fin@openthegift.com.

I hope Julian's story transported you, evoked emotion, and challenged your sense of wonder. If you have not read my other novels, please check them out. Want more *Managed Series* jewels? My FREE short story (with the long title) "Rhodium Tycoon: Olin Ou's Legacy Unraveling the Enigmatic Rise of the Madras Motor" is found only at my website, finlaybeach.com

Toward Truth,

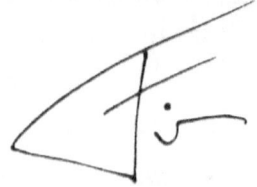

finlaybeach.com

Continue the Adventure

also by Finlay Beach

Managed Paranoia – Book One

—

Managed Paranoia – Book Two

—

Managed Paranoia – Book Three:
The Series' Explosive Conclusion

—

The Seventh Pawn
A Managed Paranoia Prequel

—

Rhodium Tycoon: A Short Story

www.ingramcontent.com/pod-product-compliance
Lightning Source LLC
Chambersburg PA
CBHW031427200626
46814CB00016B/2675